# FINDING CRISTINA

Emilia Rosa

D1518757

To my parents Hermenegildo and Eva.

*Gracious young ladies, fashionable young bucks,*
*Escape the streets, the overwhelming dust;*
*You'll find no better places for picnics*
*Than in Copacabana.*

*Verses from the "Jardim Botânico" trams, circa 1905. In História*
*das Ruas do Rio, Brasil Gerson*

# CHAPTER 1

The early sunlight plunged its fingers into the cobalt-blue sea—the sea the Portuguese explorers thought was a river. It sprinkled the wave tops, exploded with a myriad of diamonds that crashed upon the coast's soft sand. Slowly the light spread toward the sidewalk where little black and white stones mimicked waves and sand. The sun reached the asphalt then reflected against the relatively sparse large houses that fringed the thoroughfare, facing the sea.

The beach is Copacabana; the thoroughfare is Atlântica Avenue; and the sidewalks, in the future, would become the symbol of that Brazilian city: Rio de Janeiro. Rio, the city where dwell the *Cariocas*[i]—the Tamoio indians' word for the stone house the white man built around 1503 on the mouth of the homonymous river.

Inside one of these houses, a young woman wandered about its quiet living room. She had a beautiful kimono of flowery silk tied low on her hips and contrasting with the simple, cotton pajamas she wore. Her beautiful face had a thoughtful expression. She had sold as much as she dared: the crystal, some of the precious Russian silk shawls, the entire silver service. . . what now? Dismiss Maria? She could not possibly let her go! Cristina was a baby when a sturdy, blond, fifteen-year-old Maria Petronilha Specht came to work for her parents, and now she was a member of the family. It was so comforting to see her smiling face every morning. Besides, she trusted Maria completely to take care of her

1

mother. Cristina practically had to force her to accept the insignificant salary she could afford to pay; it was almost a token. Still, the housekeeper used part of it to pamper her mother with little luxuries, like flowers for the breakfast tray.

Well, she would have to forbid Maria to spend money on flowers. But not today, she decided, determined not to allow the growing sense of distress to overtake her. No, today Maria would still decorate her mother's tray with flowers, she thought, with a feeling that if she could keep control of these small domestic details, everything else would be fine. She just had to find a way to convince her mother that selling the house was the sensible thing to do. There was no way progress could be stopped—history had proven that plenty of times. So why not be practical and benefit from it? And it would be wonderful to live in an apartment in a tall building with a view—just like the people in Manhattan, she thought, dreamily. Although, she doubted there would ever be such tall buildings in Copacabana. And in Manhattan they could never have the stunning view of Copacabana beach! She sighed with the longing one feels for something unknown, but idealized, and shaking her head as to dismiss that dream, quickly went to her mother's bedroom.

Through the open window the cool, early morning air barely caressed a pair of white lace panels that filtered the early sunlight coming into the bedroom. A pale shade of pink covered the walls and complemented the gilded frame that wrapped a large reproduction of Vasily Perov's *Easter Procession in a Village*. In a corner, over a tall chest of drawers, the gently swaying flame of a votive candle illuminated the features of a Madonna. In the opposite corner, the mirror of a vanity reflected the bed, where a woman lay propped on two large silken pillows, her silhouette framed by tall bedposts. Her long, gray hair was tucked inside a white nightcap made of delicate lace that matched her bed jacket.

"Good morning, *matushka*." Cristina kissed the woman's brow. This was one of the very few Russian words she had learned, her parents, Vasili and Sonya Abramov, having insisted she learn Portuguese, since that was the language spoken in the country where they had chosen to live. "Did you have a good night's sleep?"

Her mother smiled when she saw that Cristina was wearing

the gift Daniel had given her last Christmas. Such a personal gift could only have one meaning—which the silly child had not understood. "Yes, my dear, thank you. And did you have a restful night?"

"I did, mother. Slept like a log," she smiled contentedly while dropping onto the bed alongside her mother. She then changed the subject: "That builder contacted me again."

"Please, let us not dwell on that again, my dear," her mother gently cut her short.

"But, mother, by selling the house we would solve all our problems." Cristina's large eyes scrutinized her mother's face.

"This is the patrimony your beloved father left you, my child," Sonya answered in her thick Russian accent, her hand automatically stroking one of the tassels that finished the corners of the pillows.

Cristina had embroidered those precious pillows for her while still at school. Sonya and Vladimir had made sure their girl went to a good school, so they sent her to the already prestigious Sion. The school was located at Marquês de Abrantes street, less than a ten-minute walk from their prior abode at Barão do Flamengo Street, in the Flamengo neighborhood. There, from eight in the morning until five in the afternoon, she learned classic languages, French, piano, and embroidery, as it befitted young ladies. But she also assimilated a ladylike behavior, which unwittingly trickled down to the girls from their aristocratic mother superior, Mère Dieudonnée. Cristina's fluency in English came from her daily contact with the daughter of their American neighbors, who, during all the years they lived in Flamengo, was not only her playmate but also attended the same school.

Cristina bit the end of the pencil and bent her head forward, hiding from her mother the distress her beautiful eyes betrayed. Her fashionably bobbed hair fell alongside her cheek. To her mother's chagrin, she had recently cut her long locks *à la garçonne*, what Sonya imputed to a fashion fad. But in reality Cristina's silky black tresses were now part of some lady's coiffure; she had sold them to a wig maker who had paid good money for the beautiful hair. That did not stress the young woman, however, who knew that eventually her hair would grow longer.

Her mother always said her hair was as black as her

3

grandmother's, but Cristina had had to resort to a creative mental exercise to construct the image of a grandmother she had never known because her parents had no pictures of their ancestors. With a small amount of money inherited from a distant relative, they had left Russia at the beginning of the century, and, after a brief period in Portugal, established themselves in the city of Rio de Janeiro—and that was as much as she knew of their past. She had concluded they had not been happy in Russia since they did not like to speak about life there. In contrast, they had always seemed very content in Brazil.

"I cannot come up with more cuts in our budget." Cristina shook her head impatiently and the dark hair swayed, like a fringe of soft threads of silk. With an absent gesture, she smoothed the pink chenille spread on the bed.

In recent months, Cristina had sold the beautiful sterling silverware—inherited from their obscure ancestors; they so seldom used it anyway. An upstart couple for whom she had worked several times, playing the piano, wanted to throw an elegant dinner party—elegant by their *nouveau rich* standards, anyway—and their somewhat depleted set matched hers almost perfectly. Happily she saw the gorgeous silverware find a new home therefore allowing her to settle a number of impending bills. Next to go were the crystal carafes and vodka shot glasses. Vladimir had kept a variety of Russian vodka in his well-stocked bar, which he pompously poured from these beautiful carafes, collected since Cristina was a child. As the only one who drank alcohol had gone to join his ancestors, the objects had no use, so she sold them without giving it a second thought.

"You know what I think," she said after a pause, and then continued, full of energy. "We would be smart if we sold the house and went to live in a snug little place. Or, if you would like, I could barter with the construction contractor for a nice unit on the top floor. Can you begin to imagine the view of the beach we would have, mother, from the eighth floor?"

Sonya seemed unmoved by her daughter's excited speech, but she did not stop her. Cristina took hold of her mother's hand and traced the blue veins visible beneath the skin with one delicate finger.

"An apartment building is not the end of the world, mother.

Actually, much higher buildings—they call them skyscrapers—have been built all over the world," she said, admiringly. "Besides, we cannot stop progress; we will soon have apartment buildings right here in Copacabana."

"My dear," Sonya cut her off with a firm voice, "I would die rather than leave you without a decent inheritance. Your father would have been mortified at the thought of selling this house so one of those monsters could be built in its place. He was thinking of you when he built this house. Let us try to keep it. We will find a way, I know," she pleaded in a softer tone, giving Cristina's hand a light squeeze and patting the girl's cheek.

Cristina was unable to repress a small sigh, but she forced a smile. "Yes, we will find a way. I should not have worried you with this anyway." She rose from the side of the bed where she had been sitting and bent to kiss the woman on the cheek. "Well, I am going to finish dressing. And I guess Maria is about to bring you breakfast."

"Oh, Cristina, please tell Maria no more flowers, will you? It only eats up our budget and I never cared much for flowers anyway," Sonya added quickly before the girl could dismiss her request.

"Mother, you know Maria gets them from her admirers at the open market," she giggled and pirouetted out of the room, leaving a smile on her mother's face.

As the door closed behind Cristina, Sonya's smile faded. Less than a year ago her husband had died after a brief but devastating malady. He'd had several small strokes until the last one left him almost completely paralyzed, and in a few days he was gone. She knew the hospital bill had not been small, but as Cristina had kept from her the extent of it, she had no inkling of the import of the total cost. She ignored that it had consumed most of what they had. Since her husband's death, she had been in an enfeebled state, battling depression though trying to convince herself that she must live, for the girl would be left alone in the world. Except, of course, for the faithful Maria. But what could Maria really do to help? Oh, if only she could join her Vladimir certain that Cristina would be cared for by a husband, Sonya thought sadly. That excellent Daniel, she was sure, wanted to propose, but what would the hardheaded girl do if he dared? She

5

had silly romantic ideas of only marrying for love.

Humph, love, she thought, dismissively. What did it matter, after all? She just had to think of that poor Countess Dobrinsky— her sad affair with that Brazilian—and for what? Love! The Countess's first marriage, arranged by her family, had been very unhappy, she granted. But on the other hand, she and Vladimir had been matched by their families back in their village in Russia, and they had had a wonderful life together. And so did all her neighbors and relatives who had been matched. Unfortunately, it seemed her Cristina was too imbued with these ideas of love and would never consider marriage as a means to stabilize her situation, as any sensible woman should. To make matters worse, the girl had gotten a job downtown and had taken to playing for parties and the like, thought Sonya, shaking her head with sadness. It troubled her that a young lady with her ancestry had to work for money. Ah, if at least her father had accepted her... And with these somber thoughts, Sonya rested her head against the pillows. She sighed deeply and, shutting her eyes, settled down as her mind wandered to happier times, when Vladimir was still with them.

* * *

Cristina's eyes suddenly focused on her wrist where the gold chains of a bracelet shimmered. No, she couldn't possibly sell that too! Her mother had gotten it for her when she was born, so selling it was quite out of the question. And how much would she get for something with incalculable sentimental value? Besides, she had no idea what kind of stones those really were. No, she told herself, something would come up. But not if she was late to work, she realized after consulting her watch, and rushed to her bedroom to finish dressing.

Over the cream-colored silk dress, a hip-length, red linen jacket with white shawl collar was cinched just below the waist by a wide belt. The large white pockets carried everything she needed: money, a cambric handkerchief, and the house keys. The white, pointed shoes tied with a red ribbon completed the look. A red cloche hat was firmly pinned to her hair. From beneath its brim she peeked at her image in the mirror and stuck out a tongue at it and smiled. She quickly poked her head through the kitchen door to bid

Maria goodbye, then her Louis heels resounded on the parquet, the front door slammed, and she was gone.

\* \* \*

February in Brazil, and especially in Rio, meant Carnaval, when many took vacations; there was much revelry, and more drinking than usual. But over the next few days, while most people enjoyed themselves, Cristina would be working at parties, playing the piano to amuse the revelers. Another weekend working, she sighed at the thought while making her way to Nossa Senhora de Copacabana Avenue. There she stood with other people in one of the many islets that, at regular intervals, punctuated the center of that thoroughfare. After a short wait they all boarded the electric tram that would take them to the downtown station of Largo da Carioca.

Her economic situation was foremost on her mind; no matter how much she tried to avoid it, selling the house seemed to be the best option. Her father always advised her that the best thing to do in a difficult situation was to let time pass and a solution might present itself. It was not postponing, he would explain, but allowing events to take a natural course. Hasty action, he had told her often, sometimes precipitates what could have been avoided by allowing a little time to pass and perhaps point to a solution.

With that in mind, she tried to focus on the passing images of the city instead of dwelling on her problems but shifted in her seat as another image, one that had been lingering in the back of her mind, insinuated itself into her thoughts.

Earlier that morning, as it was her habit, she had gone for a brisk walk on Atlântica Avenue, along Copacabana beach. It was always so soothing to watch the waves, the seagulls gliding and frolicking in the water. She always enjoyed studying the black and white undulating mosaic of the sidewalk, made of small cubes of Portuguese stones—black basalt and white limestone—a visual metaphor for the waves. Now, instead, the presence of a man overshadowed everything else.

For the last couple of weeks, she was perplexed to see him, almost daily, and in different parts of town. He never addressed her, and she could not attribute the encounters to anything else but chance. He never approached her, nor could she tell for sure that he ever looked at her more than casually. Yet she started to grow anxious in the anticipation of seeing him.

Every morning there he was, sitting on the edge of the sidewalk, facing the sea. Invariably he puffed on a cigar, and an open paper partially blocked his face. In the distance she could see the bluish smoke curl around him until a gust of breeze stole it into the crisp morning air. That very morning during her stroll she had finally admitted to herself that she longed to take a good look at him. But as her steps took her closer to him, she refused to turn his way. She could see him from the corner of her eye, and to her intense dismay, it seemed that he was oblivious to her presence.

She had been so distracted by these thoughts that she started when the tram arrived at the busy downtown square, the Largo da Carioca. She alighted hurriedly, crossed the streets, and soon reached Casa Carlos Gomes, number 47 at Carioca Street, where her job was to perform on the piano music pieces the customers were considering for purchase. She had just sat at the piano and raised the fallboard when the manager placed a sheet of music in front of her.

"Miss Abramov, a customer would like you to perform this."

She was pleased: it was Ernesto Nazareth's romantic waltz "Eponina." It was one of her favorites, together with "Carioca," both by that most *Carioca* composer, and written in 1913. So, she thought, not everyone in Rio wanted her to perform only Carnaval music. Curious of whom the customer might be, she took a peek, but when their eyes met, she saw the stranger, the very one she had been thinking of for the last half hour.

He was observing her—he was actually looking at her. And that look weighed on her almost physically. She decided to concentrate her attention on the sheet in front of her, in an attempt to ignore his eyes. Still, she felt flustered, and her fingers seemed heavy upon the piano keys, but she was still able to play well. Meanwhile, the stranger signaled the manager not to interrupt her, and went to the cashier. When the music ended, she looked up, and, with an odd mix of dismay and relief, realized that he was gone.

For the rest of the morning, her thoughts were constantly

on the stranger. Requests from other customers did not help to distract her, as she had hoped. It started to exasperate her that a complete stranger could take over her mind so intensely. And by the time she was ready to leave for lunch, she had developed a warped sense of injury toward the man with whom she had never even spoken. She would be loath to admit what really bothered her—that although the stranger seemed to always be in her path, he never showed the slightest interest in her. Conscious of her beauty, she knew how much she attracted all eyes, yet that man seemed impervious to her charms. Well, actually today he seemed to have noticed her, although, truth be told, his eyes betrayed no emotion—and *that*, for some inexplicable reason, had piqued her and added to the unreasonable feeling of aggravation she felt toward him.

Walking hurriedly she arrived at Confeitaria Colombo, her favorite place for a quick lunch. The moment she entered the place, she saw him—the stranger—sitting alone. His cigar resting on an ashtray, he held a newspaper, which he did not read because his attention had been on the entrance door. Cristina marched straight to his table, her eyes never leaving him, and without thinking fired a question with no preamble.

"Would you care to explain why you have been following me, sir?"

The stranger stood up with a white napkin in the grip of his hand. His athletic stature towering over her, he bowed a silent greeting. Awaiting a response to her question, she analyzed the tanned face turned down to her. The strong jaw line was softened by a beautiful mouth, the corners of which softly curved in the shadow of a smile. From the carefully combed hair, a disobedient curl had escaped, which gave him a somewhat boyish air. He was dressed in an impeccable cream linen suit and brown shoes that shone like mirrors. He looked at her with a puzzled expression, and it further exasperated her that her sudden attack had not disturbed him. His blue eyes seemed to consider her dispassionately, and she thought she actually saw a twinkle of amusement in them—oh, the provoking creature!

"Well, I am waiting for your explanation," she insisted in a commanding tone, hiding her restless hands inside her large pockets. His eyebrows went up for a fraction of a second, and he forced back a budding smile.

"I am sorry, Senhorita," he answered in Portuguese with a very thick accent. "My Portuguese is...limited," he said in an apologetic manner. "Would you mind repeating that...slowly?"

His voice had the effect of a sip of warm chocolate that spread insider her, and she felt her whole body softening. An engaging, frank smile of perfectly white teeth completely disarmed her. His eyes, steadily on hers, also seemed to smile.

"Do you speak French?" she snapped back in that language.

"Not really, I'm afraid. Perhaps you speak English?" he tried in terrible, halting French.

"Very well, English then!" And she repeated the question in English.

What a delicious accent, he thought. She was more enchanting in close quarters than he expected. Those sparkling eyes, daring him to respond, they actually teased his feelings. Her little mouth puckered in the most delicious pout, like two ripe strawberries that he felt an urge to taste. A soft, telltale sigh escaped his lips.

"Well," she insisted, assuming his sigh betrayed boredom.

"Oh, my manners!" And he quickly pulled out a chair. "May I invite you to join me, Miss...?" His eyes pleaded for a truce.

"My name is Cristina, but I do not think I should join you, sir," she added hastily, taking a small step back. "After all, we have not been formally introduced. I only approached you to find out the reason why you are always in my path everywhere I go. Rio is a large city, you know, and I have never yet seen someone so many times in such a short period of time! So, why are you following me? Who are you?"

Adorable, he thought. And this time the amused expression in his eyes was unmistakable and hers flashed in outrage. The buzz of conversations, the constant comings and goings of patrons, and the cries of the waiters inside the busy pastry shop at lunchtime kept their conversation somewhat private.

"Please, allow me to introduce myself. My name is Robert Laughton." His melodious voice once more caressed her ears. And before she could notice, he deftly seized her hand and smiled. "Delighted."

At his touch, Cristina felt like a small electric shock

discharge in her stomach, yet she relinquished her hand to him, somehow mellowed by his soothing touch. As their eyes met, what was left of her anger ebbed away. With that most chivalrous, yet simple, of gestures, he had caught her unprepared. Yes, he was a gentleman. But still, she suddenly reminded herself, it did not change the fact that he *was* a stranger.

"Sir," she quickly added, "that does not change the fact that...."

"Yes," he interposed with a charming smile. "I am a stranger, who seems to be always in your way. But have you considered that we just might frequent the same places simply because of taste? Yes, this is a big city," he added, "but it seems to me that some of the places you frequent are also of great interest to foreigners. And, as a foreigner, they naturally attracted me. Does that not sound simple enough, Miss Cristina?"

*The places you frequent*—she thought her heart beat a little faster. That could only mean.... So he did see her, although he seemed never to look at her? Perhaps she was not just a dim face in the crowd, after all, and the thought somehow improved her mood.

While speaking, he had pulled out a chair and maneuvered her by the hand he had kept captive in such a way that, without realizing it, she was sitting down.

She had been disarmed and outmaneuvered, and—what was worse—by such a simple explanation. The childish tale she had so elaborately created in her fertile mind—handsome foreigner preying on young woman with sinister intentions—had fallen to pieces, dismantled like those sand castles she used to build on the beach as a child. Suddenly, the ridiculousness of her position hit her: she had accosted a perfect stranger to interrogate him on actions she could not impute to him. Oh, God, what might he be thinking of her? And that thought made her blush.

"I realize I have acted like a child." She lowered her eyes hiding her confusion. "Please, accept my deepest apologies," and she began rising to leave.

He had been completely seduced by her candor and felt tempted to confess the whole truth; but the thought of the mission that had brought him to Rio enabled him to control that impulse. No, he could not. At least not yet.

"Please, do not leave," he said as his fingers touched hers

momentarily.

The soft inflection in his voice detained her. His eyes reflected the frank smile that parted his lips. And there was no mocking in his eyes; they were friendly, inviting.

"Would you join me? Have some coffee, or maybe you would prefer tea?" As she agreed, he called the waiter and ordered tea in his broken Portuguese. "This is such a beautiful town. What an incredible chain of mountains. I can imagine what the Portuguese explorers thought when they first saw it."

"They actually thought it was a river." And as he looked surprised, she added: "Hence the name: Rio de Janeiro, river of January."

"I went to the Corcovado," he told her. "Such a beautiful view of the city from there. Especially in the evening."

Yes, she had seen him there and now, by the way he looked at her, with the light of a smile in his eyes, she knew he had also seen her. She lowered her eyes absently contemplating her fingers twirling the spoon in the cup. But when she raised the cup to her lips, their eyes met and she felt that something had happened. Somewhere inside her emerged the absolute certainty that life would never be the same again—and that peculiar thought somehow soothed her. She set the cup down and leaned back feeling as if she were in the company of an old, dear friend. How odd.

"You have to agree it is a bit unusual that I see you almost every day when I go out for my morning stroll, Mr. Laughton," she pressed, in a feeble attempt to fight that comfortable feeling of intimacy.

He took a long puff of his cigar, then letting out the air slowly, he smiled at her. "Perhaps," his eyes acquired a teasing expression, "like you, I also enjoy the early maritime air."

Cristina could not help laughing. "You have a very peculiar way to make things look so simple."

"Because, my dear young lady, they *are* simple."

They both laughed and for the next forty minutes—the remaining length of her lunch break—they delighted in conversation. Robert learned that she was very intelligent and had a tremendous interest in life in the United States. That her beauty was striking he had noticed the very first time he saw her, even from afar. But that it should be coupled with intelligence, he did not expect. The beautiful women he had met so far were vain and, quite frankly, uninteresting. He was surprised to a certain degree and recognized that, for the first time in his life, he enjoyed the intellectual company of a woman and felt compelled to keep her interest aroused. He sipped his coffee and enjoyed the exchange with that beautiful and bright girl, all the while observing her attentively.

Seeing her from close quarters, he realized her eyes were not dark blue—as he had thought them from afar—but were an astonishing violet hue that turned almost black when she was upset. Her hair, half hidden under the cloche hat, was tar black and seemed soft as silk. He wondered about its scent, how it would feel to the touch. Her clothes were not of the latest vogue, but they were very well kept and she carried herself with a natural regal elegance—just as her mother might have done at her age, he surmised. To an unaccustomed eye, these details would have passed unperceived, but not to him, used as he was to dealing with the most fashionable flappers of New York.

What was happening? He had a moment to question himself and felt alarmed at the fast and unconscious way in which he had become enchanted by her. This was not one of those empty-headed flappers with whom he could have a passing infatuation.

Soon, he chided himself, he would be running after her like a puppy if he let his barriers fall. But, he wondered, did he really want these barriers up?

While they chatted she managed to eat all the delicacies on her dish. Pastel was a kind of dough folded over ground beef and deep fried—it seemed to be a favorite, for she had eaten four. Then she attacked a couple of sweet pastries. Quindim, Portuguese in origin, she explained: a concoction made with egg yolks, shredded coconut, and an abundance of sugar that made Robert shudder at the thought. God only knew how anyone could enjoy such sweetness without getting sick in the act of consuming the things!

"My mother says I have a gigantic worm inside my stomach that devours everything I eat," she said and laughed.

She had a charming way of tossing her head back and narrowing her eyes when laughing—and such laughter, so joyful and sincere. Was it that mix of Russian and Brazilian blood, or was just that this one had a special way about her? The truth was that he was finding it harder and harder to keep his distance from her.

Cristina was also attracted to him, and the more they talked, the more comfortable she felt. It was strange, she thought, as if she had known him forever.

After a glance at the clock on the wall, she said: "Oh, I must go or I will lose my job," and she suddenly stood up.

She adamantly insisted on paying her share of the bill and parted company. For the briefest instant she seemed to hesitate, and then was gone, a graceful doe making her way through the maze of tables, chairs, and people.

He had not mentioned meeting her again, she thought, disappointed. Well, a man like him—she had no doubt he was wealthy—would certainly run like the devil from the cross, as the Brazilian saying went, upon learning of her financial troubles. To top it off, she had a sickly mother at home. No, it was better this way; we should not meet anymore, she thought, knowing full well that this was not how she really felt. Why see him again, get attached, and then suffer? Yet the very thought of never hearing his voice or seeing his smiling eyes made her heart sink.

Try as she did to avoid it, the whole rest of the day she kept thinking of him. She remembered the first time she saw him, at the Corcovado Mountain. Before dusk, Daniel had taken her there to see the city lights. She had noticed Robert as soon as they arrived—that tall, blond Apollo towering above everyone was impossible to miss. She had tried to keep her eyes and thoughts concentrated on the city lights below, a view she loved, but that had suddenly lost its attraction, and her eyes kept wandering to Robert's handsome face. And then Daniel had insisted they leave.

# CHAPTER 2

D aniel… She felt sick to her stomach—not for how much she had eaten at lunch but for sheer disgust at the thought of him. On the way down to the city that evening, they left the tram that took them from the top of the mountain to its base and got back into his car. While riding, he suddenly steered from the road to a secluded area and parked. She had been thinking of Robert and was so distracted that she only realized what was happening when, with shaky hands, he awkwardly pushed a small blue velvet box into her hand.

"Oh, Cristina, Cristina!" his voice a whisper suffocated by emotion. She thought he looked even paler than normal, if that was possible. But before she could say anything, his clammy hands grasped her shoulders and pulled her to him. Her head was forced backwards as he crushed her lips with his hungry mouth, as though he wanted to devour her. She was suddenly shaken from her reverie—and so vividly the feeling still lingered that she shuddered, but more with disgust than outrage.

She had managed to push him away, and a well-applied cuff to his face brought his groping to a halt—and some needed color to his cheeks, she later thought, chuckling. He was a comical figure, the poor man: startled eyes, eyeglasses midway down his long nose, rubbing the injured cheek tenderly. She thought he seemed more stunned by the strength of her hand.

"Oh, Cristina, my love, I was overtaken by my feelings," he scrambled to explain in a thread of a voice.

"Overtaken…by your…*feelings*," she gasped. "You animal, how dare you? How dare you? What kind of . . . ." Anger constricted her throat and impeded her speech. Eyes blazing with indignation, she glared at him. He shrank back, fearing another cuff, one hand still holding his cheek.

"Are you out of your mind, you…you…what kind of woman do you think I am? Take me home immediately," she demanded, in a shaky voice. Outrage displayed by the queen of England would not have matched hers.

Overwhelmed and overpowered, crushed, feeling miserable in his failure, Daniel could not find anything to say and took to the road again. He stole a few sideways glances at her, but the storm was still evident, and at the possibility of another explosion, he decided to keep his eyes on the road. What a bearcat, he thought. It was only when the car stopped in front of her house that she finally realized she still held the blue box in a tight grasp. Mechanically she opened it and saw a sparkling ring.

"I…wanted to…propose…to you," he stammered not daring to look at her.

"So that is how you propose to a young lady, you scoundrel? Be glad I will not tell anyone of your conduct. Imagine if they knew of it in the Music Institute. Imagine how my mother would feel if she knew of your behavior. Don't you dare ever cross my path again," she said in a low, menacing voice, and threw the box at him in rage.

She left and slammed the car door with all her strength. His dreams shattered, Daniel left after Cristina entered the house. Who would have thought that a proposal of marriage would have been received as something so offensive, he wondered.

\* \* \*

As Cristina appeared at the kitchen door, Maria turned to her, and her eyes widened in surprise. "Jesus, Mary, and Joseph! What happened, child? You been robbed?"

Cristina darted into the kitchen, and collapsed onto a chair. When she could finally speak, she described what had happened with Daniel on their way down from Corcovado.

"All the souls in Purgatory," Maria mumbled. "Who'd have

thought such behavior of Daniel, always so meek, so discreet!" She shook her head in disbelief.

"I forbade him to approach me again," Cristina added in a self-satisfied tone.

"Your mother was so hopeful you two were going to marry."

"Maria," Cristina grabbed her hand, "not a word to my mother." And seeing that the other hesitated, added: "Promise!"

"But, how am I supposed to hide it from her? She's going to ask about Daniel when he doesn't come over. He always comes to visit her."

"I'll think of something. Give me some time, but for the moment, I do not want to bother her unnecessarily."

"Very well. Now, drink this." Maria handed her a glass of sugared water she had been preparing while Cristina talked. "It'll help calm you down—you're too excited."

Cristina took the glass but held Maria's hand against her cheek and leaned her head against the woman's crisp apron. It was comforting to inhale the scent of starch, which brought back memories of her childhood.

"How I wish I was still a child. Things were so much easier then."

"Oh, but you grown up a mighty pretty woman, and men are all falling over each other to propose to you, my pretty." She nodded her head in agreement with her own statement.

"Believe me when I say I could live without this kind of embarrassment," Cristina sighed. She thought of the events she had just endured of which her teacher—a man her parents had always trusted, whom she considered as an older brother—was the culprit. But all of a sudden, the ridiculousness of the situation struck her. When she turned to Maria, her eyes were beaming, the color back to her cheeks. "You should have seen his face when I slapped him."

Suddenly both women burst into peals of laughter. "Now that it is all over," Cristina said between eruptions of laughter. "Oh, the poor man…" She could not go on, overtaken by spasmodic giggles. She buried her face in her hands, almost crying. "Shh, shh! We don't want mother to hear us, Maria." Cristina tried to stop Maria by holding a hand to her mouth.

"What was the joke?" Sonya's voice suddenly echoed in the kitchen.

Their faces congealed with an expression of surprise as Cristina and Maria were abruptly brought back from their cheerfulness.

"Mother, are you feeling well?" Cristina asked, steadying her voice and discreetly wiping the tears away.

"I heard the laughs and wanted to know what was so amusing." She looked from one to the other with questioning eyes, her eyebrows raised and on her mouth an expectant smile.

"But why didn't you ring the bell?" Maria leapt to her feet. "Sit down and I will make you a nice glass of passion fruit juice." Wrapping an arm around Sonya's shoulders, Maria guided her to one of the chairs. "That will help you have a nice night's sleep."

In the meantime Cristina had slipped out of the kitchen, saving herself from giving explanations.

"Yes, I'd like that. But I want to be told the joke too. By the way you two were laughing, it has to be something truly funny."

"I'll try to tell it, but I am not very good at it, you know." And Maria wracked her brain searching for a joke to impart.

\* \* \*

During the week that followed her confrontation with Daniel, Cristina was amazed at the lengths to which a guilty heart would go to seek forgiveness. Anyone could have told her that the gestures were actually those of a man in love.

When she arrived home after work that Monday, she found a bouquet of purple hyacinths and a card with a brief message: "Forgive me!" Tuesday brought another bouquet, now of red carnations, and the message was: "My heart aches for you." On the following day, she was surprised to find a third and enormous bouquet of daisies encumbering her chest of drawers; its message: "My love is loyal." By Thursday she merely shrugged her shoulders when another bouquet lay alongside the other three— glorious primroses and the message "I can't live without you." On Friday she just stood there and cocked a wary eye at the red roses adorning her night stand. Only this time, somewhat to her disappointment, they carried no message.

"You modern young people don't know nothing," Maria teased. "Where I come from, girls knew the meaning of flowers. Red roses mean *I love you*. So learned a young lady, but knowing nothing of the language of flowers, humph. You must admit, Daniel does not give up so easily. The man really loves you, my girl. He persists despite your resistance." Maria winked at Cristina and went back to her ironing.

"Well, *I* don't love him," Cristina followed her and snapped back. "He can persist until he is blue in the face because it will not change my mind. I cannot imagine being with him," and she shuddered at the thought of his lips mauling her delicate mouth, of his bony arms crushing her body like a boa constrictor.

"He has sent your ticket to the opera tonight, as always," Maria said, referring to the envelope she had left on the table in the entrance hall.

"I saw it. The way you placed it, I could not have missed it even if I was blind."

"Are you going? He'll probably want to drive you there."

"Oh, he wouldn't dare! Unless he wants his cheek *massaged* again!" She chuckled with immense pleasure at the recollection.

"Ah, but what if it was the handsome foreigner sending those flowers?" Maria asked with a mischievous twinkle in her eyes.

"Maria!" Cristina sprang out of the chair she had been sitting in. "If you say one more thing about him, I will never tell you anything again!" Irritated, she regretted the moment she had decided to confide in Maria.

"Oh, now don't you go starting one of your long, angry monolobes. Bring your dress to me, instead, if you want it ironed."

"It is 'mon-o-logue!'"

"Bah, monolobe, monologue, it's all the same." She gestured dismissively and resumed ironing. "Humph. These learned people like to teach us ignorant folk all those fancy words, but they don't know nothing of life. Now bring the dress here. Then you can sit by and go on ranting."

Cristina turned on her heels, cheeks flushed, suppressing the urge to set Maria straight. Later, she thought, she would set her straight later! But later she would have forgotten that she had been upset: her anger always died quickly, nevermore to be remembered.

When she entered her room to get the dress and saw the five vases of flowers, she heaved a huge sigh and could not help shaking her head in disbelief. Would Daniel send another bouquet the next day? Well, the good side of it was that, if he did, she could always open a flower shop, she thought with scorn, and stuck out a tongue at the flowers. But really, she hoped he would quit. His behavior was positively ridiculous in showering her with all the stupid flowers. But they smelled good, she thought, bending to one of the bouquets and enjoying the perfume exuded by the red roses. Maria was right, she admitted; she would have reacted differently if the flowers were from Robert. She shrugged her shoulders and left with the dress, not giving another thought to Daniel—although thanks to him she would have a couple of hours of good music in her near future.

"Be careful with this dress, will you? This is silk," she admonished Maria, handing her the dress.

"Oh, you are now an expert in ironing too, are you? Perhaps I should step aside and let your learned self take charge of this difficult mission," Maria mocked, as, with hands on hips, she stepped away from the ironing board.

As a response Cristina made a face to her and bursting with laughter decamped to her room to finish her toilet. There she reached for a bottle of Chanel No 5—the only perfume she used, and only for evening events—and pressed one drop behind each earlobe. She liked the story of the perfume: among the several fragrances created by Ernest Beaux, her perfumer, Coco Chanel, chose number five—her lucky number. That bottle was Daniel's gift for her 20th birthday, one year ago. It had certainly cost him a fortune, since he had to get it from France. At that time she was stunned at his gesture but never suspected an ulterior motive. How naïve she was that she never suspected this man wanted her.

\* \* \*

Daniel had spent that week tormented by Cristina's silence. All the flowers he had sent and no word came his way. He decided to conveniently *catch* the flu, an excellent excuse for skipping work that week so he could spend his time watching Cristina. He meant to hide a mark on his left cheek that suspiciously resembled a hand. So each morning he followed Cristina from the distance, without being noticed, while she went for her stroll at the beach. He thought that he could somehow guess her feelings for him, even without talking to her. But it was torture, nevertheless, to watch her and not be able to address her and make her understand how much he loved her—no, how much he had always loved her!

That Friday he followed her to the Confeitaria Colombo and saw her with a stranger—the same one he had first seen at Corcovado and who seemed to be everywhere. While he observed them sitting there, chatting so contentedly, he had to restrain himself not to accost them and…and…and what? What *could* he do? Punch that wall of a man? Of a small frame and quite short, he would certainly be crushed like a flea by that Herculean specimen. The man was probably over seven feet tall, the troglodyte! He wisely dismissed those thoughts and decided to lie in wait and observe. Only later, after Cristina and then Robert had left, he approached the young waiter who had served them to see what he could learn.

"The muscular big shot is an American," the waiter responded to his inquiry. "I never see him with anyone; he's kind of a loner. Today was the first time I saw him with that jane. She eats here almost every day. Works round the corner," he signaled with his thumb. "Her name is Cristina. I always serve her. What a pretty lil' thing, jee!" As Daniel did not make any comment, but seemed very interested, he continued. "Anyways, the only other person I've seen with the American is the private dick who has an office not far from here."

"Dick?" Daniel repeated the word, puzzled.

"Yeah, dick. Ya know, private investigator."

"Oh, I see!"

"Tall fella, comes here to get his lunch sometimes; name is Ramires. Well," the waiter seemed to consider, "not as tall as the American. Anyways, odd-looking bird, easy to recognize: long face, long nose, and a pair of thick eyebrows with an even thicker moustache," he gestured, mimicking the brows and moustache, as if it would help Daniel understand him better.

As the waiter's source of garrulousness seemed to have drained away, Daniel reached for his wallet and started to pull some notes out of it while asking, "Anything else come to mind about the...private dick?"

The waiter threw a glance to his right then to his left, smoothed his pomaded hair, and tucked the notes that were handed to him into his apron's wide pocket, trying to calculate the amount by its thickness. It proved to be a miraculous tonic that helped revive his memory.

"As a matter of fact, this Ramires is a regular fixture at the Bar Adolph, a joint on Assembleia Street," he said while dusting the table top with his napkin. He smiled ingratiatingly and continued, "Well, people actually know it as Iron Arm. That joint has a curious story, if you're interested."

Daniel could not have cared less about the story why it was called Iron Arm, so he interrupted the waiter. "Thank you, but the information you already gave me is satisfactory."

"Can I bring you a cup of coffee or something? The boss is already checking on me." With his head he motioned to where a stout man stood, keeping an eye on the whole place.

Daniel thanked him and quickly left, wondering why the American was meeting with a private investigator. He decided he had to find a way to accost this Ramires and unravel the mystery. It might be to his advantage; the American might be involved in some shady deal, and it would gain him favor to expose him to Cristina. He went home to get ready for the Theatro Municipal where, he was sure, he would find Cristina—and, who knows, might even be able to approach her and try his luck with an apology. After all, he had smoothed the path with flowers, and, he thought, what woman didn't have a soft spot for flowers?

* * *

After Cristina had gone back to work, Robert finished his cigar and left Colombo. What a picturesque city, he thought while he walked through downtown to Ramires's office, not far from where he and Cristina had had lunch. Despite the terrible summer heat coupled with high humidity, the walk was still very appealing. Or maybe it was the fact that a certain young lady lived in Rio that made it all the more interesting.

The astrologer of the Portuguese king Dom Manuel had once said that Brazil would one day be "the refuge and shelter for the Portuguese peoples." In 1807 his prophecy came to fruition when Napoleon's army marched through Portugal. On the morning of November 29th of 1807, escorted by British ships, the king of Portugal Dom João VI, his Spanish queen Dona Carlota Joaquina, and their court—about ten thousand people scattered among a convoy of some two dozen ships—started their trip to the faraway colony of Brazil. They found refuge in Rio where the court was then established.

The wave of modernization that hit the city at the dawn of the 20th Century had left a few buildings intact, raw scars amid sanitized, modernistic stucco walls. Did Mayor Pereira Passos's constructive angst miss these pariahs? Or did he decide to spare a few of them, like a farmer who plows the field but leaves a few trees untouched? Lost in time, hidden in dark, irregular alleys with cobblestone pavements, some buildings had been spared, decrepit and silent relics from the Portuguese court.

With their roofs of ceramic tiles and white-washed walls, these colonial structures concealed humid alleys. Rooms were kept cool by force of darkness provided by wooden shutters. The original latticed *muxarabiê* windows, similar to the *mashrabiya* from the Arabs, no longer existed, except in the depictions of Jean Baptiste Debret of that long gone time.

Quaint as this part of Rio might have seemed to tourists, Robert preferred modern cities, like The Big Apple, as Jack FitzGerald, the horse-racing columnist for *The Morning Telegraph*, once called New York. Its tall buildings, busy traffic, and streets crowded with people with urgent goals were the perfect setting for his energetic soul. The city's constant hum was a paradigm of evolution and progress, of man's victory over matter, and he so loved the virile power it exuded.

After several minutes of walking at a slow pace under the oven-like heat of the tropical sun, he was more than ready for a break. When he got to his destination and entered the building, the cool air was a blessing. Although it carried a musty scent, it was a vastly welcome contrast to the torrid heat outside. Up the narrow stairway he reached the second floor. At one of the doors, a somewhat discolored sign read *"Ramires, Detetive Particular."* He removed his hat and dried the perspiration on his face with a white handkerchief.

A muffled *"Entre!"* answered Robert's knock, so he entered the private investigator's sanctum. It was a small room, with grayish walls that had once been white, where a couple of hooks precariously held a wrinkled jacket and a hat. The place was encumbered with a large desk, littered with papers and large files. The rest of the furniture consisted of a couple of mismatched wooden chairs and a large, also encumbered, bookcase. Through a gap in the half-opened window panes, a solitary ray of sun penetrated the room. The light, impeded by objects, imprinted deformed shadows upon the walls.

Behind the desk a man in shirtsleeves, his collar removed and hanging limply on the back of his chair, read a few pages held in his hands. His knitted, bushy eyebrows betrayed the effort he put into the task. Perilously, at his right elbow, sat a bottle of beer and a dish with a half-eaten sandwich, its crumbs scattered on the table. As the door closed behind Robert, the man tore his eyes from the pages and revealed a thin, equine face, where a bushy moustache seemed to compete with the eyebrows for domination.

"Mr. Laughton," he said in a raspy voice and thickly accented English. As he sprang up, he extended a long, bony hand with thickly joined fingers. His hairy arms emerged from sleeves that had been sloppily rolled up. For a moment he observed the contrast between his hand and the one it grasped—large but well formed, tanned with well-cared for nails. "I was just reviewing a report for your father before taking it to the Postal Office."

They both sat down and Robert carefully placed his hat on what seemed to be the desk's only clear spot.

"Well, in that case I will spare you a trip—and the postage." Robert held out a hand. As the man hesitated, his eyebrows shot up and a grin twisted his lips. He withdrew the hand and sat back, his eyes scrutinizing the man's face. "Unless, Mr. Ramires, you do not trust me." He spoke slowly, a half joke, half serious statement.

"Mr. Laughton," Ramires retorted, shifting uncomfortably in his chair, "of course I trust you. "Here," and he handed the pages to Robert. "This is the latest report. Maybe you could read it to your father over the phone."

Without looking at them, Robert folded the pages and tucked them into his pocket. "Now, Mr. Ramires, let us talk business. I believe this concludes your job." The man seemed surprised. "You unearthed all the information pertinent to my father's inquiries; therefore, your work is done. I am quite satisfied and I know my father will be too." Ramires's lips curled in the caricature of a smile. "And since you did an excellent job, you deserve a bonus." He took a thick envelope from his jacket and tossed it across the desk. "Please, verify that this compensates you for your time and expenses."

"I am sure it does." But Ramires did not touch the envelope.

"Well," Robert rose from the chair, "since both parties are content, I thank you for your excellent job and will bid you a good day, Mr. Ramires." He adjusted his Panama hat, bowed slightly, and left the room.

Futz, thought Ramires, where was he going to find another golden goose like this? He had thought he could milk the man a little longer. That put the brakes on his hopes! But he knew what was bugging the American, and his yellowed teeth flickered through the bushy moustache: he was sure the American was carrying a torch for the looker. Ramires opened the envelope, wet his fingertips on his tongue, and counted the bills. When he finished he whistled. Well, this had been some swell deal. He knew what he was going to do with all that jack. First, he would buy himself some new threads, Then, on Saturday he would get all swanky, go to the Adolph, get some drinks, and find himself a skirt with a nice pair of pins—not exactly in that order, he guffawed. Well, if that sheba—what was her name? Oh, yes, Dulce—if Dulce was at the Adolph, he thought while smoothing his mustache, then his night would be swell.

He reached for his hat and jacket and, whistling a tune, left, pleased with how bright the near future looked.

\* \* \*

Cristina sat in one of the red velvet-upholstered chairs in the audience of the Theatro Municipal.

"Excuse me," she heard from a nearby voice.

She turned her head to find one of the young theater-ushers standing beside her. As she assented, he handed her a creased paper. She read the message scribbled in black ink by a quick hand: *Miss Cristina, I would be honored if you would join me in my box. Robert.* Her heart quickened. She gave the boy a puzzled look, and he pointed to one of the boxes to the right of the stage. She followed the direction of his outstretched arm and, even at that distance, recognized Robert, who nodded at her. She felt a tug at the base of her stomach: beside him a flaxen-haired woman watched her through opera glasses. The young usher invited her to follow him, so she quickly tucked the message inside the small purse hanging from her wrist and went to join them.

She followed the usher through the corridor to the boxes dreading the moment when her eyes would find Robert's, yet longing to see him. Her heart pounded so loudly she heard it above the din of the conversations. As they neared the door, it opened, and there he was. She did not think it possible, but her heart beat even faster. He wore an impeccably cut evening tailcoat, certainly made to measure, judging by how perfectly it fit him. The immaculately white, starched shirt contrasted beautifully with the tanned skin of his strong neck. The only jewelry he wore were the small diamond-incrusted studs that closed his shirtfront, repeated in the gold cufflinks. His hair shone with perfumed brilliantine, the persistent curl now successfully tamed.

"Welcome." His soft voice was enchanting, and with an intense feeling, she realized how much she had longed to hear it. His sparkling blue eyes searched hers for a brief moment.

Inside, in the dim light of the box, she saw two men standing up and a woman sitting who, with opera glasses in hand, scrutinized the audience. It was the woman Cristina had seen beside Robert when she had looked up from her seat. Her heart leaped. Was this woman with him? Worse yet, was she *something* to him? Having no right over him, she tried to suppress these thoughts.

"Come in and meet my party. This is Lady Desiree, my cousin, Miss Cristina," he started the introductions.

Cousin, Cristina thought, holding back a sigh of relief. And her relieved expression had not escaped the sagacious young woman who had turned her face to look at her. She smiled with the same frank expression as Robert did.

She stood up and a hand of long, thin fingers took Cristina's in a warm grasp. She was tall and thin, her delicate limbs moving harmoniously. Her large, round, gray eyes had a teasing expression. A tiny nose delicately sloped up at the very tip, and her china-red lips had a constant upward curl at the corners. One small dimple in one of her rosy cheeks made her face look very young— a sharp contrast with her sophisticated attire. Her dress—a Madeleine Vionnet, most assuredly, Cristina concluded—was of black silk satin with a low, draped back. At the waist a pearl-embroidered ellipsis set off lines of pearls that crossed through bodice and skirt. Her pearl-studded shoes, of the same fabric as the dress, were André Pérugia's. An enormous ring—a rectangular aquamarine surrounded by pearls—and an immensely long string of pearls around her neck complemented her attire.

"Robbie," Desiree protested, still holding Cristina's hand in her own and turning to her cousin, "your friend will have the wrong idea of me. She will think I am nobility or something." Her voice was soft, melodious, and Cristina fancied it was a feminine version of Robert's. "Darling," she added, turning back to Cristina, "my name is Desiree. My cousin likes to play with the fact that I am a commoner who married into English nobility." She let go of Cristina's hand, the smile lingering on her lips.

"And that brings me to the nobility in question," Robert said, turning to one of the men who stepped forward and took hold of her hand. His smiling, pale gray eyes examined hers, openly inquisitive. "Maximillian Oscar Walston-Armstrong, Earl of Bembrock," he mocked in an English accent and added with a flourish, "Miss Cristina."

"Charmed," the man said and bowed. "But you must call me Max, as all my friends do. And since you are a friend of Robert, consider my wife and I yours, too."

He was a little shorter than his wife and seemed older than her. But perhaps this illusion was increased by his bald head and Desiree's extremely young looks. Like Robert and the other gentleman, he also wore formal evening attire.

Robert had now turned to the anxious little man standing in awe of Cristina. He had an abundance of jet-black hair, tamed by an also abundant amount of brilliantine. His eyebrows were of the same tone and lavishness, as was his curled mustache. He had a bluish chin and upper lip, the result of a voluminous beard that he sometimes had to shave twice on a single day—being a fastidiously fashionable man. Anyone who saw the caricature of Portuguese diplomat Luís Pinto de Soveral, 1st Marquis of Soveral, would find a resemblance between the "Blue Monkey" and this gentleman. Soveral had gotten his sobriquet from the then-Prince of Wales, later Edward VII, for the same facial characteristic.

Before Robert even started to speak, the man cut him short.

"Jean-Louis Lagisquet, *a votre service, Mademoiselle*," and he bowed deeply. When Cristina answered in French, his admiration seemed to deepen, and he passionately took her hand into his.

"As I was trying to say, this is our good friend Spigot, Miss Cristina," Robert interposed, amused by his friend's enraptured expression.

"*Espigot*," the Frenchman corrected, using the French vernacular, and addressing Robert with a scorching look, all the while maintaining a hold on Cristina's hand. Then his expression changed completely and, turning a pair of tender eyes to her, he asked in French: "Are you French, Mademoiselle?"

"Oh, no," she answered in the same language. "I had a very good teacher, that is all. She was French, you see. I recall that she was from Bayonne."

"*Tiens*, but that is why you speak such marvelous French: your teacher was from Gascony, like me," he beamed. "I am from Saint-Jean-de-Luz, not too far from Bayonne," he said and placed a heartfelt kiss on her hand.

"Now, Spigot," Robert interrupted, "that is enough." And taking a light hold of Cristina's elbow, he steered her away from his friend. "Do not flirt with the young lady so openly. It will certainly embarrass her."

"*Oh-lá-lá*, Robert," he struck back in English that had a thick French accent, "you are jealous because mademoiselle does not mind my flirting, hein?" His thick eyebrows shot up to give more weight to the challenge as his whole body stretched, and he seemed to grow taller. He then turned a cheerful face to Cristina: "I am sure Mademoiselle is not offended because I could not resist her beautiful little hands," and he once more took hold of one of her hands, quickly touching his lips to it.

"You did not offend me," she laughed, delighted with his flamboyant ways. It was adorable how he pronounced Robert's name with a French accent.

"Did you hear Mademoiselle, Robert? What do you think now, hein?" And his face rose to Robert's in a challenge.

"What I think is that I will have to keep you away from the lady. Now sit there and hold your hands tight."

And in saying so, he poked the Frenchman's chest causing him to loose balance, and land on the nearest chair. Robert then turned to Cristina, who watched the scene in amusement, and piloted her to the chair beside his cousin's. He explained to Cristina that Spigot had gotten his nickname during the Great War as he had a special flair for finding good wine. The first choice of name from his airmen comrades had been "Barrel," but since the Frenchman was slim, "Spigot" he became, as, because of him, the excellent wine of the country of France flowed abundantly, to his friends' great delight.

Robert pulled a gold watch out of his pocket. "It is almost time." He then found a place behind Desiree which allowed him to turn to the stage while surreptitiously observing Cristina.

"Max, darling," Desiree said to her husband, who was seated on her right, "may I have a drink?"

"Of course, m'dear." He searched beneath the tails of his jacket where a pocket was hidden, and handed his wife a hip flask. Desiree unscrewed the top and carefully poured the amber liquid into a thimble-like cup.

"Would you like a sip, Cris?" she asked Cristina.

"Thank you, but I do not really like alcohol."

"Oh, dear," Deisree chuckled, "this is not alcohol, darling. I can't drink alcohol," and she smiled and drank from the cup, then refilled it and drank twice more.

"She has a problem ingesting alcohol, you see," Max interposed. "Her delicate stomach."

"Darling Max, always trying to protect me," she said, turning to him with a loving glance. "Yes, I think you could put it that way, but my *intolerance* is called alcoholism," she answered,

29

amused at Cristina's embarrassment. "Don't be embarrassed," she said, patting the girl's hand. "I am actually a recovered alcoholic, so you can congratulate me. Max carries this hipflask in case I feel thirsty. This, for example," she said while screwing the little cap to the flask, "is cold British tea." She returned the flask and brushed a finger on her husband's cheek. He held her hand, placed a kiss in its palm, and closed it, letting it go.

"You are too quiet back there, Spigot," Robert teased his friend, and four pairs of curious eyes turned to the French man quick enough to see him dreamily gazing at Cristina.

"Oh, I was just enjoying the view," he sighed, smiling at Cristina. "These Brazilian ladies… I am afraid I will lose my heart to them," he confessed, ignoring the amused faces turned to him.

Suddenly the curtains opened and their attention shifted. But somehow Cristina could not keep hers on the stage. The certainty that behind her, Robert would be watching her, made her self-conscious, unable to keep her attention on the scene. Yet it did not bother her—on the contrary. Rather, she felt excited and, at the same time, it gave her a sense of comfort from the fact that they were in the same room, in such proximity of each other. She imagined his blue eyes on her, their intense look scrutinizing her, and it actually made her shiver. Had he noticed, she wondered, apprehensively. It was then that she realized the magnetism he already exerted on her by simply being near. How could a man she barely knew hold such sway over her and so quickly? What was it? Was it his gaze, his voice, or the touch of his hand that drew her to him? Perhaps it was something else. Something good and steady emanated from his eyes that had reached her from the moment they had first met. He was like a tall mountain set on solid base, steady, so self-reliant, it seemed. But what was it that lay hidden on its summit, she wondered dreamily while the music played in the background.

The applause startled Cristina, so engulfed in her thoughts that she had not seen the end of the first act. And when her eyes met Robert's, she knew he, too, had been miles away from there, perhaps lingering in the same dreamy world as she. He smiled and his face shone with the light that filled his eyes. Then the enchantment, the golden thread that had held them under the same spell, was broken with a loud yawn from Spigot, who sprang up, stretched his limbs, and energetically began to discuss the music with Max as both headed for the door.

Robert smiled at her, scraps of their secret communion still lingering in his expression. "Would you like something to drink?" he asked in a low voice that made her heart jump inside her. What was it that every time this man opened his mouth she wanted to bask in the sound of his voice, like in the sun she loved so much? Cristina wordlessly nodded her assent to his question. He placed an order for drinks, excused himself to the ladies, and followed the two other men, who had gone outside to smoke.

"This is a beautiful dress you are wearing, Cris. I seem to recognize it," Desiree said and frowned, observing the dress carefully. She was sure she had seen it before. The lacquer-red silk was gathered at Cristina's hips where a large bow let hang a long string of golden threads. Its squared bodice was supported by thin straps and revealed her beautiful shoulders. As she moved her arms, the sides were exposed and showed embroidered leaves and flowers that were repeated on the hem. "I know: it's a Worth," Desiree exclaimed, and clapped, delighted. "I have an incredible memory for this kind of thing, you know.'"

"Actually, I copied it from a magazine. I would never be able to afford it," Cristina smiled.

"Then you are lucky because you must have a wonderful, very skilled seamstress."

"I meant that I did it myself," Cristina clarified.

"Well, I can't believe it! And—don't tell me—you embroidered it, too?" At Cristina's assenting nod she marveled. "What a talented young woman you are," she marveled. "I, on the other hand, can't sew on a button to save my life." And, turning to Robert who had entered with a glass of refreshment for Cristina: "Robbie, can you believe this young lady sewed *and* embroidered the dress she is wearing? Isn't she incredibly talented?"

"Yes, Miss Cristina is very talented," he said and his eyes twinkled at Cristina. Then sweeping an admiring glance at her dress: "I am not versed on these matters, but the dress not only becomes you immensely, it is beautifully crafted." He turned to his cousin. "Did you know she also plays the piano—admirably?"

"You don't say! Well, maybe we could convince her to join us for dinner tonight, Robbie," Desiree told her cousin. "Perhaps she might give us the pleasure of listening to her play."

Robert looked at Cristina with pleading eyes. "I actually meant to invite you. Can I prevail upon you to join our party later tonight? We promise that you will not get home too late, right, Desiree?"

"Absolutely, darling," and turning to Cristina, "Cris, please, say yes."

The smile Robert flashed at her would have been enough to convince her, Cristina thought. "Well, I guess…yes," she agreed, but added quickly: "So long as I don't get home too late. I have to wake up early tomorrow."

"Do not worry," Desiree took upon herself to answer for Robert. "Robert will make sure you will get home before midnight, Cinderella." Desiree smiled at Cristina and patted the girl's hand.

"Do you need to wake up early for work tomorrow?" Robert asked.

"Well, I do have work, but in the evening—I play at a party. But, no, I like to accompany our housekeeper to the open market. Maria is like family for us, and I have done that since I was a little girl. She likes to be there early, around seven in the morning."

"*That* early!" Desiree was shocked. "Oh, I am so lazy and slow in the morning, unlike my energetic cousin here. I guess business men have to wake up early, although I doubt it *needs* be at six o'clock," she teased him. "He not only beats the roosters out of bed, but spends one hour exercising with Bunky. Bunky is his sidekick," she explained, but seeing that Cristina did not understand, explained further: "Bunky has basically raised Robbie; he has tamed the little beast for Uncle John," and she turned to Robert. "Check out this chest, these arms." She giggled and tried to squeeze Robert's biceps.

"Desiree, you are embarrassing our guest," he said and gave Cristina a boyish smile, which, again, made her heart melt for the hundredth time. "I apologize for my cousin. She can sometimes be like a child."

"Oh, darling Max," Desiree turned excitedly to her husband who had just returned with Spigot. "Cris will join us tonight, and she promised to play something on the piano!" The fact that Cristina hadn't had an opportunity to agree to play did not occur to

Desiree, who, like a butterfly, moved from person to person without stopping long.

"Marvelous," Max responded, and Spigot took the opportunity as to thank Cristina and hurriedly press a kiss on her hand.

"Merci, merci, mille fois, Mademoiselle! I am sure these little hands play like a fairy." He then turned to Robert: "And don't look at me with that menacing expression because I am not afraid of you!"

Robert could not help but laugh for Spigot looked very much like a little fighting rooster. "Now abate that fire—else Spigot will have to be put under a spigot to cool down."

"Eh, flyboy, you want to fight *le grand Espigot*?" he mocked back, folding his hands into fists and holding them up. "You know these hands have done much damage in their lives. Want to try them?"

"I say, both you boys quiet down," Max whispered. "The curtain is rising. Find your places and shush!"

\* \* \*

At the theater's entrance the task of hiring cabs was relinquished to Cristina, since Robert was unable to fully understand the Brazilian drivers. They were doubly fortunate that evening, because one of them was Ananias, a cabbie she had known for years, and he could communicate in English well enough. To this one she entrusted the men, since Desiree suggested the men follow them in a different taxi so the ladies would be more comfortable. Cristina was puzzled at Robert's request to be driven to the harbor.

"*Ingleses*?" the driver of the car asked, giving her a wink as she entered with Desiree.

"Yes, they are English. But *I* am Brazilian, so don't you play smart because I know how much this should cost," she told the crestfallen man as the car started to take off.

Robert had reluctantly agreed to the separation, uneasy at the idea of Desiree having time alone with Cristina. God only knew what his cousin might be telling the girl, he thought. He knew her too well and was sure she was up to something—and he had an idea of what that *something* would be. She had a penchant for matchmaking, although she had never actually matched anyone, but that small detail had never stopped her from trying. Besides, his bachelor life was too good. And then there was Bunky—that cross to bear, courtesy of his father. No, definitely, he did not feel ready yet to walk the middle aisle.

This year he would be twenty-eight and was too frequently hearing repeated his father's story—of how at that age he had already been married for four years. He knew the story of his parents' meeting so well that he thought he could repeat it backwards in his sleep. His father and his cousin, Desiree's father, met the French twins, Anne Louise and Anne Marie at the 1893 Columbian Exhibition, in Chicago. A couple of years later, they married, against the wishes of the girls' family. Robert was startled from his reverie by a loud laugh; he had not noticed that Spigot and Max were having a good time teasing him about Cristina.

"So, the pretty little Brazilian mermaid has harpooned your heart, no?" Spigot ribbed him. "Look at him, Max, already dreaming about his beautiful bride!"

"I say, Spigot," and Max slapped Robert on the shoulder, chuckling, "the old boy's heart has been captured more securely than the helmet on Keiser Wilhelm's head," and he and Spigot burst out laughing.

Robert thought he had made a big mistake by choosing to sit in the back with those two silly buffs, so he did the best he could to remain cool when, in fact, he'd have liked to wring both their necks. But the effect was the reverse. His demeanor excited the two men and their teasing redoubled. He leaned to the front and decided to try to start a conversation with the driver, despite his poor knowledge of Portuguese.

"Happy fellas," the driver winked at Robert and grinned, signaling the back seat with his head. "A bit too much booze, huh," and he mimed drinking with one hand.

"No, it's just their brains made of scrambled eggs," and he laughed at the man's puzzled look but chose not to try to make himself understood. "Never mind, just drive us to the harbor." He sat back, and resigned himself to the teasing.

\* \* \*

"Flyboys," Desiree repeated. "That's what they called the aviators of the American Expeditionary Forces during the war, flyboys," she explained to Cristina. And as the car stopped at a light, she took hold of her little mesh handbag and, pulling out the tiny vanity case, started to powder her nose.

"So, Robert was an aviator?" Cristina queried with surprise.

"You probably remember that the US entered the war in April of seventeen. Well, my cousin could not wait to join the army and try to get himself killed by a German bullet. What better way than as an aviator, right? I guess the idea of going down in flames appealed to him," and she shrugged. "He was 21 then. He was never an ace, like Rickenbacker, but since he was quite good, he came back unscathed—well, with a few bruises and cuts, but nothing really serious," and she put the compact case back into her purse. "But let us not talk about the war—and thank God it is over. I want to know about you. How did you and Robert meet? He drives me mad being so secretive and all that," she lamented and continued talking, not giving Cristina a chance to speak: "He never tells me anything—and he and I were raised like brother and sister, mind you! My mother and his were sisters. They were both French—twins—and each married an American and moved to the States. I don't recall Robbie's mother much; she died young. His father, John, was my father's cousin. Anyway, we lived in the same building, next door actually, and, I don't know, maybe their closeness brought Robbie and me together." She shrugged her shoulders. "Anyway, we are four years apart." She suddenly turned to Cristina, a twinkle in her eyes. "Would you believe Mr. Robert Laughton used to drop on all fours so I could play cowgirl?" They both laughed, Cristina trying to imagine a young Robert playing horse with a child on his back. "I would scream at the top of my lungs until he agreed, just to shut me up. Then I'd force him to parade me through the whole house. And, of course, as I was a cowgirl I had to tame him, so he had to act like a wild horse. He put his foot down at the spurs, though," and she and Cristina burst out laughing. "Oh, I was a pest, you can't begin to imagine how much. My father had these spurs that belonged to his grandfather, and one day I got it into my head that I *had* to wear them and ride Robbie! Of course I didn't get my wish, luckily for him," she laughed. "Since I can remember, Robbie was always in charge, solving little problems we kids had, putting an end to fights—oh, I was a tomboy and fought anybody who crossed my path!"

"I can hardly imagine that. You seem so sweet and gentle," Cristina said, surprised, her thin eyebrows arched.

"Yet I was a beast. Robbie once saved a cat from me; I was trying to send the poor animal flying in his toy airplane from the top of the building! He, of course, got scratched badly," she laughed. "No wonder he used to call me 'Little Scourge of God.'"

By the time the car arrived at the harbor, both women were laughing so hard at Desiree's childhood stories they were almost crying. The car door was opened and they joined the gentlemen.

"We just have to take the launch now," Desiree told Cristina.

"Take the launch?"

# CHAPTER 3

"I guess my cousin forgot to tell you that we are all staying on Robert's dad's yacht. See those lights?" She pointed to the dark mass of water where, in the distance, a few bright dots of light illuminated a yacht. "That is the *Anne Louise*, Uncle John's yacht. He named it after his wife," she told Cristina. "My mother was Anne Marie."

"Is your mother alive?"

"No," was the laconic answer. She turned merry eyes to Cristina, "Look at that! I wanted to know more about you and the whole time you steered the conversation and made *me* talk, you smart little cookie. Never mind, we'll have time to talk later."

The cab drivers were paid and Robert retained the one who had driven Cristina and his cousin; he gave the man a hefty sum and asked him to stay there because he would have another passenger in a few hours. He told the man it would be worth waiting. Then they all embarked on a small launch moored at the harbor's edge. Its white hull cutting through the calm platinum water, the vessel travelled quickly, and in just a few minutes they boarded a large yacht, intensely illuminated.

Without delay the five took to the stairs, crossed the deck, and went below. In the dining room, on a table covered with a white linen tablecloth, crystal and silver sparkled in the light of two tall candles that had just been lit. The wood-paneled walls were softened by off-white silk curtains rippling on the portholes, now wide open to allow in gusts of the sea breeze. A centerpiece of white calla lilies filled the table and contributed to the general sense of coolness. What a coincidence, my favorite flowers, thought Cristina. In one corner, a black baby grand piano created an eye-catching contrast.

As Cristina could not stay very long, without preamble they approached the table and Robert helped her with the chair on the right of his seat, at the head of the table. Desiree motioned Spigot to Cristina's right, seating herself on Robert's left, her husband taking the seat beside her after helping her with her chair.

"What a beautiful room." Cristina's eyes traveled around the room and rested on the large marine oils, representing naval battles, placed around the walls.

"Those were my dad's only contributions and, to his surprise, met with my beloved cousin's approval," Robert said, following her gaze. "Desiree is responsible for the decoration of this room."

"You decorated this room?" Cristina asked Desiree.

"She actually decorated the whole thing, top to bottom— even the kitchen. As a matter of fact, she decorated dad's apartment, too," he added as an afterthought. "If I let her, she would turn my cave—as she calls my little apartment—she'd turn it into some micro-Versailles, with lots of silk and frills and God only knows what else," he laughed as Desiree grimaced at him. "But I put my foot down and she was only allowed to interfere with my father's real estate."

"And what is wrong with Versailles, can you tell me?" Spigot questioned. Then without waiting for an answer, he resumed the task of savoring some champagne that had just been poured into his glass.

"Robert should allow a feminine hand into his cave," Max interpolated. "I say, there is nothing more relaxing for males' eyes than a home decorated by a woman, old boy. Especially a sophisticated woman, as in this case."

"Well, hopefully he will soon have someone to do his decorating." Desiree glanced at Robert with a mischievous look.

Robert turned to Cristina, after giving Desiree a warning look: "So Miss Cristina, you approve of my cousin's decorating abilities?"

"Oh, I most definitely do. This room has been beautifully

decorated. You have wonderful taste, Desiree," she continued, admiring the room. "I can only imagine how beautiful your home is."

Robert sputtered a laugh and Cristina turned to him, surprised. "These two live in a hotel," he explained. "The sweet young lady facing you across the table could never find a place to suit her taste. And she has the most patient husband in the world."

"He is a darling," said Desiree, turning to her husband and blowing him a kiss, which he captured on the air and deposited on his lips. "So," Robert continued, "the happy couple lives in the penthouse of a hotel in Manhattan. She has never decorated a table that belonged to her—let alone a room—because everything is done by the hotel staff."

"*Oh là-là*, and very beautifully, Mademoiselle, I assure you," Spigot suddenly interrupted. "What?" he queried, challenging Robert's critical stare. "It is a beautiful suite," he insisted, then, dismissing Robert, turned his attention back to the champagne glass quickly being emptied.

"As I was saying before being interrupted," Robert continued, turning to Cristina, "she needs not do anything. Imagine that even a pet the hotel has—a cat named Billy—so she doesn't even need to get one herself because the little beast is a constant visitor at her suite." They all laughed and he continued, "And so she goes around bossing people—yes, this gentle soul you see there," and Desiree batted her eyelashes repeatedly and assumed what she judged to be a naïve expression. "She goes around telling her poor victims what to do with their homes, while living in a hotel! So my father's bathtub—as she calls it—fell victim to her eager, little hands."

"Well, someone's got to do the dirty job, thank you very much," Desiree stood up and, taking a bow, turned away and walked to the phonograph. Soon Enrico Caruso's voice filled the air with Rossini's "Crucifixus" from Petite Messe Solennelle.

"Oh, no, not again, Desiree," Robert protested. "I think I can sing this aria in my sleep!"

They all laughed at his disheartened expression.

"Max could sing too," Desiree smiled at her husband. "You both have nice voices. But, no, neither of you could ever be a tenor like Caruso. There will never be another Caruso; he was unique."

"Yeah, I know, I know," Robert mocked, winking at Cristina.

"*I* have a beautiful voice," Spigot chimed in, setting his empty glass on the table with a decisive gesture. "As a matter of fact, when Mademoiselle Cristina plays tonight," and he bowed his head at her, "I could join her and sing, if she would allow me."

"Oh, yes. That is all I need: to end my night with your squawking voice piercing my poor ears," Robert broke into laughter while Spigot's chest swelled in outrage. "Please, I beg you, have pity on us!"

"Max and I saw Caruso before his death," Desiree addressed Cristina before the French man could start a heated tirade. "On Christmas Eve of '20, we saw him in the Metropolitan. He interpreted Eléazar in 'La Juive'—remember, Max?"

"How could I forget, my love? He was sublime." Max shook his head with a deep sigh. "What a loss."

"He was my father's favorite. He used to listen to him almost every evening, after dinner," Cristina said.

"Well, after all this talk of Caruso, I know my cousin will make Carusos for all of us after dinner," Robert told Cristina.

"And I hope she will," Spigot retorted, his tone a bit dry, still sour for not being able to remonstrate at Robert earlier, but his eyes already starting to twinkle at the thought of a cocktail.

"Although I don't drink, I am sure Cris will enjoy my Caruso," she turned a bright smile to Cristina, who had been amusing herself by quietly following their exchange.

"For my part, I adore it," Spigot interposed quickly, before Cristina had a chance to answer.

"Sure," Cristina added. She did not appreciate alcoholic beverages, but how could she answer otherwise without being unkind to Desiree's clear efforts to please her?

"Don't worry, I will help you with your drink if you can't finish it," Robert whispered near her ear while in the background Spigot lauded the qualities of that concoction. It had not escaped him that the girl did not look as excited about the drink as she tried to portray.

At Robert's warm voice, his lips so close to her ear, a frisson went through Cristina's body. She turned her head to him and her soft eyes rose to find his; the depth she saw in their blueness attracted her. His gaze searched her lips and traveled back to her eyes. She swallowed hard, her nostrils flurrying slightly, disturbed by the feelings his nearness brought; it amazed her how deeply it touched her. For a fraction of an instant, she imagined his lips on hers, tasting the flavor of his mouth, the texture of his yielding flesh. But the fleeting moment was gone as they both averted their eyes; dinner was being served and the distraction was never more welcome than to Cristina.

The dinner progressed with pleasant conversation. The food was simple but delicious: cold roast of beef with horseradish mayonnaise, and a crisp Caesar salad with juicy slices of cantaloupe and papaya for dessert.

"Your cook was especially inspired today, Robert," Max said at the end of the dinner. "Actually, he has never been so inspired, I dare say. This roast is sublime, old man."

"I have a new cook, didn't I tell you?" he answered casually, while he finished his dessert.

"A new cook? Since when?" Desiree asked.

"Since today. I guess I told you my other cook was behaving oddly. So when he asked me to be released, well, I just did it." He shrugged his shoulders at his cousin's startled expression. "Look here, what did you expect me to do? The man had wanted to leave for some time, so I paid him and he left. I don't see what the big deal is. Wasn't dinner good?"

"Excellent," Spigot interjected quickly, "exquisite, *absolument délicieux.*"

"And how did you find this new cook, I mean, being in a foreign country and all?" Desiree chimed in, ignoring Spigot's remark.

"I met him the other day, quite accidentally, when I was having lunch downtown. It was a very interesting lunch," he smiled and glanced at Cristina, who lowered her eyes to her glass. "He heard me asking the waiter if he knew a cook, and he came forward."

"You picked someone out of the street and brought him here without knowing who he is?" Desiree was surprised.

"I guess if you were my father, you would not have hired Bunky," he countered, which she answered with a withering look. "Anyway," he continued, "Eugênio was assistant to the chef of the

British embassy. The man has quite an impressive résumé. In fact, the last ambassador wanted to take him to England. They all loved him there. I called the embassy and got it all from them," he added, seeing it was not enough for Desiree. "In fact, I want you to meet him," and he turned to the young woman removing the dishes. "Could you please tell Eugênio I would like to see him?"

"Eu...Eu... what?" Desiree asked, intrigued.

"Eugênio," Cristina pronounced slowly and smiled at Desiree's knitted eyebrows. "I guess Eugene would be the English version of the name?"

"So the man is Brazilian and can cook like that? No offense," she turned to Cristina, "but I never imagined a Brazilian cook would be able to do" and she gestured with both hands, encompassing the table, "to cook something so simple but so delicious. I mean, the man does know English taste, does he not, Max?" And Max limited himself to a nod, busy as he was with chewing the last of the dessert on his dish.

"I have worked for the British embassy playing the piano at some of their dinners," Cristina explained, "and they always fed me afterwards. The chef actually left most of the cooking to Eugênio, who he trusted absolutely. I should have recognized his touch. Eugênio is very talented and quite the character, too," she added.

As Cristina finished speaking, a blond man entered the room. Desiree was spellbound. Blond! But weren't all Brazilians dark-haired?

"Mr. Laughton," he addressed Robert in English with a mixture of British and Brazilian accents. He then bowed to the rest of the company. A moment after he entered the room, a bull terrier calmly followed him in.

"What a cutie," Desiree cooed and craned her neck to better see the animal.

"Tony!" The cook hurried after the dog, but the animal defiantly walked away, smartly dodging his grasp by creeping under table and chairs. "I am so sorry, Sir," the cook apologized, embarrassed. "He probably sneaked out of the kitchen when I left."

"No harm done." Amused, Robert watched the dog. Since his first moment on the yacht, Tony had captivated him and proven to be a discreet and quiet passenger, and, like his owner, happily keeping to the kitchen quarters and only making quick visits to the upper deck. Robert owned a Boxer, a breed of dog that kept their impressions to themselves, and Tony presented the same quality.

"His name is Tony?" Desiree asked. "How cute!"

"Marc Anthony, to be more precise, but Tony to his friends, I was told," Robert answered noticing the dog's intelligent glance at him.

Tony suddenly stopped beside Cristina and sniffed the air. Raising his muscular chest, he unceremoniously rested his paws on her lap, greeting her with a recognizing growl, his tail merrily wagging.

"Tony." She petted his head and rubbed his back, "How are you doing? Yes, I missed you, too," she added when he licked her hand.

"I gather you and Tony have been *formally* introduced," Robert said in Portuguese, low enough to be heard only by Cristina, and she turned an amused eye to him.

"Come," Eugênio firmly called to the dog. "Have you no manners? Come here right now and leave Miss Cristina alone!" He slapped his thigh, urging the dog to join him.

Either Tony did not want to mar the good impression he had previously made, or the mention of his lack of manners worked on his pride, but the fact is that he left Cristina, and slowly, as if making the point that the decision had been his, marched across the room and sat down beside Eugênio. Then, forgetting his poise, yawned loudly and began to methodically scratch his ear, as even the best mannered dog sometimes needed an energetic scratch. Content, he licked his lips and directed his attention to the five pairs of eyes watching him, his ears raised to attention.

"You wanted to see me, Mr. Laughton? Was there a problem? Was the dinner not to your expectation?"

"No, everything was delicious, thank you, Eugênio. Actually, the excellence of your dinner was the reason I called you." The man smiled, pleased. "My guests showed surprise that a Brazilian would be able to cook a roast beef that could please an Englishman, and I wanted to prove to them that such phenomena existed—you are living proof."

"Are you really Brazilian?" Desiree questioned him. "I mean, you are blond, with such white skin; you look more like a…a…German," she concluded.

"Yes, madam, I am Brazilian," he turned to her a pair of cool blue eyes. "My grandparents were from Germany and my last name is Kneip. That will explain my appearance. I was born in São Lourenço, in the extreme south of Brazil. The city was founded by Jacob Rheingantz, a German, madam. My grandparents arrived in 1859, one year after its foundation. The original settlers were all German."

"Well, Monsieur Eugênio, no matter how you look or where you came from, you cook divinely," was Spigot's excited statement.

"Yes, and I raise my glass to this," Max toasted and was joined by the rest of the party, except for Desiree who, with blanched cheeks, silently stared ahead of her.

"Thank you," he bowed. Then turning to Robert: "Mr. Laughton, if you allow me, I will retire. I have to be up very early tomorrow. I will take Tony with me and make sure he will not intrude anymore."

"Yes, do so, and thank you for such a delicious meal."

"The man looks like a replica of the Keiser Whilhelm," was Desiree's bitter comment after Eugênio had left with the dog. "These Germans," she muttered. "We better keep a watch on them. Mark my words, as soon as we take our eyes off them, they will get us all into trouble again!"

"Don't exaggerate, darling," was Max's dismissive comment.

"I agree with Desiree. It was this kind of attitude that brought us to war," Spigot added.

"I see you can speak Portuguese when the occasion calls for it," Cristina said in a low voice, while the discussion continued in the background. Giving Robert a side glance as he bowed, she added. "Although…not with a Brazilian but a Portuguese accent. How so?"

"Believe it or not, this also bears a very simple explanation," he teased her. "My father's cook, who's been with him for many years, is from Mozambique." To Cristina's delight, he pronounced the man's name—Manuel—with a Portuguese accent. "Manny, as Desiree likes to call him," and he motioned his head in the direction of Desiree, who was still engrossed in an animated discussion with her husband and Spigot about the future danger Germany represented to the world. "He taught me Portuguese…and a couple of dishes from his native village," he added with a shy grin.

Yet again, her heart warmed to Robert. "Don't tell me you cook," her eyebrows darted up and she giggled. "I can't imagine the elegant Mr. Robert Laughton behind a stove!"

"I said *a couple of dishes*," he stressed. "But, well, there are many things you don't know about me," he answered in a low voice and with a mischievous look.

Tired of the arguing over the Teutonic peoples, Desiree, overhearing their conversation, changed the subject: "Robbie cooks wonderfully, isn't it true, darling?"

Max acquiesced. "Robert would be the last one to admit it, Miss Cristina, but he *is* an excellent cook. I always told him if one day he got tired of engineering, he could open a restaurant."

Cristina wondered at Robert cooking. An interesting picture, she thought.

"And I would be your daily customer, Robert," Spigot enthusiastically remarked, while caressing his belly with a satisfied sigh.

"Well, *that* is encouraging, Frog. And judging by the way you normally eat," he gave a telltale glance to his friend's belly, "you would compensate royally for any lack of customers."

Sucking in his belly, Spigot rose and directed a glance to Desiree, ignoring the laughter. "Well, enough chatter, m'lady. Now, what about that Caruso you promised us?"

"Ab-so-lute-ly," she said mimicking a flapper's babble, and springing up went to the bar. "Help me, Jeannot, will you, darling," she invited Spigot, curling a finger at him.

"*Me voilà!* Command and I will obey, *chère dame*," and in the next moment he was standing behind the little bar's counter, kissing the tips of her fingers.

Max rolled his eyes and shook his head. That Frenchie simply could not help himself when he saw a pretty woman, he thought.

"Let's see." Extricating her hand, Desiree glanced expertly through the bottles lined up on three narrow glass shelves on the wall behind her. "First, pass the cocktail glasses," she said to

Spigot. She wrinkled her nose as he handed her five glasses. "Not chilled…Well, they will have to do," she shrugged her shoulders. "Also that glass pitcher…there. And a lemon. And a knife," she commanded, retrieving the objects as he handed them to her. She cut a few thin peelings from the lemon, twisted them, and laid them on a dish.

Cristina approached the bar and, propping herself against one of the tall chairs, observed Desiree's dexterous hands.

"Now, orange juice. The advantage of once being an alcoholic," she glanced at Cristina, "is that you know a lot about booze," she winked an eye at an embarrassed Cristina. "Very well, now pass the gin." She turned to the bar and pointed at the bottles behind Spigot, "right there…yes. Now crème de menthe— *merci*!—and the vermouth," and she rewarded the Frenchman with a charming smile. "Now, we mix one part of gin with one of vermouth," and as she spoke, she measured the liquid into a pitcher, "and a third of crème de menthe. Now, ice. No, no," she stopped Spigot before he dropped large chunks of ice into the pitcher. "It has to be cracked, first. How many times have you watched me, Jeannot—will you ever learn?"

"Oh, he knows well enough, my love," her husband mumbled behind a cloud of smoke. "He just craves the attention that comes with playing dumb."

"Jealous, tommy?" Spigot asked above the laughs that had followed Max's words and the sound of Desiree crushing the ice.

"*Now* we can add the ice." Desiree said to Cristina, who watched attentively. "Stir well and strain into the glasses." She filled four of them, pouring orange juice into the fifth. "And the last touch," she said, putting a lemon twist in each glass. "Voilà," she exclaimed, clapping her hands with pleasure. Then, handing the first glass to Cristina, she took hold of the one with orange juice. "Cheers," she toasted Cristina while Spigot took his glass. "Gentlemen," she invited Robert and her husband. Then she walked to the table to find her cigarette case and the cigarette holder.

"Strong and sweet, but not exceedingly so—just right. Perfect, my dear," her husband congratulated her.

"Cheers to you, cousin." Robert raised his glass in a toast that was joined by all the other glasses.

"Absolutely *parfait*," Spigot commented when he finally agreed to remove his lips from the rim of the glass.

"Thank you." Desiree's voice came out muffled by the cigarette she was lighting. "Cris, why don't you join me? We can have some girl talk and let the males enjoy their own troglodyte talk," she chuckled.

She walked to a very small room connected to the dining room by wide-open French doors sided by two young palm trees. A few potted tropical plants filled the back of the room. A couple of comfortable armchairs flanked a settee, the trio upholstered in grey raw silk, and made with the same light wood as the dining table, all forming an inviting nook.

Cristina had not yet touched the drink and was about to follow Desiree when Robert held her arm. The shock again, she thought, perturbed, as it happened every time she felt his touch.

"Allow me," he whispered, keeping his eyes on hers. And as she looked at him, troubled, she seemed not to understand. He motioned to her glass: "to help you with the drink?" She mechanically handed it to him, and he discreetly poured most of its contents in an empty glass on the table. "She won't suspect and I won't share our secret."

"Sit here, darling, Desiree patted the chair beside her settee as Cristina approached. "Unless the smoke bothers you."

"No, go ahead; my father used to smoke, so I am quite used to it," she lied.

Desiree remembered Cristina had not spoken about herself. Although she had done most of the talking when they rode in the taxi from the theater, in her mind it was Cristina who had steered the conversation to Robert.

"Are your parents alive?"

"My father died last year. He suffered for months. It took a toll on my mother—on all of us—but she was the one who suffered the most." Cristina quietly sipped what was left of the drink, the memories of her late father suddenly fresh in her mind.

"I am sorry." Desiree's voice was soft. "A long-suffering disease is probably more difficult to take than sudden death, I suppose. Death itself is always a tragedy, for old or young." She took a deep breath and forced a smile, letting the small cylinder of ashes she had been balancing fall into a large ashtray on the side table. Her eyes fluttered for a brief moment, and Cristina thought she saw grief in them.

"So your mother is alive," Desiree spoke up. The sad expression had quickly vanished.

"Yes. She misses my father too much," and Cristina could not help a sigh, for she missed him too. "My mother has been mostly in bed. The doctor is convinced her disease was caused by a broken heart. They were so united, my mother and my father."

"Are both your parents from Rio?"

"No, they came from Russia."

"Russia?" Desiree's glass stopped midway to her lips, her eyes wide with amazement.

"Yes, they moved to Brazil many years ago, after a relative passed away and left them some money."

"How interesting," she pondered. "But why Brazil? I mean," she looked at Cristina with an intrigued expression, "you have to admit that Russia is so far away, on the other side of the world."

"Actually," Cristina seemed pensive, "you ask an interesting question. Would you be surprised if I told you it has never occurred to me to ask them? I guess I just took for granted that they moved here, never looked for a reason." She smiled and said: "Maybe they got tired of the cold and decided to move closer to the Equator?"

"Talk about closer," Desiree chuckled. "And you? Are you Russian, too, or Brazilian?"

"Neither. I was born in Paris, just prior to their move here."

"Oh, so you are French," she exclaimed, a wide smile parting her lips. "I know someone who will love to know that," she laughed and her eyes expressively turned to Spigot, in the other room.

"Well, I was just born there," Cristina added. "I am not *really* French. I guess you can say I'm Brazilian, since I lived my whole life here."

"My uncle John, Robbie's father, has a very good friend who is from Russia. Helena is her name–Helena McCarthy. Robbie calls her 'countess.'" She chuckled: "See, I am the one who gives nicknames to everybody, but Robbie beat me to hers. She seems not to mind it, though, since she was indeed a countess before marrying McCarthy—or something like that. Well, at least she never *complained* about being called that," Desiree reflected.

"A Russian countess." Cristina seemed interested.

"Yes. I am not sure of how her story goes. My uncle knows more, and I think Robbie has some knowledge. I can ask him if you want."

"No, that is fine." She smiled at Desiree. "It is just that if she were here, in Rio, I mean, I know my mother would love to meet her. Not exactly for her title, but for being a Russian. Both my parents were employed by nobility when they lived in Russia. We know just a couple of Russians here; it is not every day she can meet a compatriot living in Rio, you know."

"Sure, I understand." Desiree's eyes lowered to her glass and she started caressing its rim with one finger. Then she drained the orange juice. The pain was there, again, she thought, throbbing, tearing her from inside, almost physical. Strange how it never did go away completely but lived below the surface. A loud laugh coming from the adjoining room made her shudder. She sprung up and turned to Cristina: "What if we were to make some music?"

"It would be wonderful," she answered, her eyes lighting up. "I would be glad to play something." She stood and followed Desiree back into the dining room.

There the men sat in animated conversation, the bluish haze from Robert's cigar dissolving into the air, dispelled by the sea breeze. Half-empty glasses that had been abandoned in the heat of the battle lay scattered on the table.

"Yes, you may have freed your country from the British," Max conceded with a bow to Robert, who nonchalantly sat in the head chair. "Still, we left behind a bundle of charred remains of a fireplace to remind you bloody Yanks of your White House, old boy." Affecting indifference, Max sniffed the rose from his buttonhole with a contented expression. Then turning to see his approaching wife and Cristina, he stood up and was followed by Robert and Spigot.

"Yeah," Robert retorted calmly, a smile curling his lips. "And then these *bloody Yanks* had to come to the rescue of your side of the world," he said as his eyes encompassed both Max and Spigot, "and save you from the Huns."

Huns? Cristina remembered she heard that word to mean

Germans.

"How was I inserted into this quarrel?" the Frenchman protested. "We did not burn your Capitol, *mon ami*," he continued with passion. "*Bien au contraire*, we French helped you, do you forget?"

"Yeah, *poilu*," Robert addressed Spigot. "The Huns attacked your country, not ours! Yet we went there to save your..." he checked himself, realizing there were ladies present, and completed with less fire than he started: "your back."

"Ah, yes?" Spigot asked with a challenging tone. "You entered the war because the Huns sank the *Lusitania* and killed a hundred or so of you Americans!" And as he said it, his face froze. He swallowed hard and sank back into the chair. Idiot, he thought, what a complete idiot he was!

Of course, Max thought, the bloody fool couldn't control his tongue! He would cut it out one day, he swore to himself.

Robert's eyes flashed to Desiree, and as Cristina followed his gaze, she saw the young woman's face pale. The air in the room had suddenly become as hard as glass, oppressive.

"Don't pay attention to them, Cris." Desiree managed a quick smile and, with a slightly trembling hand, pulled another cigarette from her case. "Every time these three get together and there is some alcohol involved, they end up with a *tour de force* on whose country is best," she finished with a head shake and a mock sigh. With a forced smile she addressed them: "Now, gentlemen, gentlemen, please, remember your manners, we have a guest tonight." And turning to Cristina: "Maybe you could play something, Cristina? After all, music sooths the savage beast, does it not?"

"I'd be delighted." Cristina sat at the little stool and opened the piano. What was happening, she wondered. She had no idea, but something was wrong, and it had to do with Desiree. While she leafed through the sheet music she found "Eponina" and warmed inwardly remembering the day Robert went to Casa Carlos Gomes and got her to play it. Enough distraction, she thought. She tried to clear her mind and decide what she was going to play. Something to calm hot tempers, most definitely, she thought. Her fingers lightly rested on the cool ivory, her eyes looked ahead without seeing, and her head slightly bowed. For a few seconds she sat in silence until, finally, as she liked to describe it, the music *chose* her.

# CHAPTER 4

When Cristina's agile fingers depressed the keys with the first notes, Desiree immediately recognized one of her mother's favorites, Debussy's "Fille aux Cheveux de Lin"—"Girl with the Flaxen Hair"—which she'd heard played so many times for her on that very piano when it was in the music room of her parents' apartment. Long-buried memories cascaded through her mind in images of her mother, her father, and Ricky. Wonderful, darling Ricky, so young and full of life, so tall and dashing. They were suddenly gone, leaving only emptiness inside her. And as the final notes were softly played, silent tears trickled down her face. Retiring to the bar to fill her glass with more juice, she furtively dabbed her eyes with the bar towel, leaving behind dark stains from her made-up lashes.

As Cristina let the last note linger, her hand slowly rising in the air like a pale butterfly, Desiree broke the heavy silence that ensued with energetic applause.

"Bravo," she exclaimed and, coming quickly towards the girl as she stood up, encircled Cristina in a warm embrace. "Robert was right, you play beautifully, darling. But you are our guest and perhaps..." She turned her red-rimmed eyes away from Cristina's surprised gaze in search of her husband. "Max will play something so we can dance, darling?"

"Yes, my love," and with a swift move he took her in his arms and kissed her lips. "What should I play, old girl?"

"The Sharlestom," Spigot called in his thick accent as he sprang to his feet and took Desiree from Max's arms. "And you, *ma belle*, will dance with me."

"Cat's meow," Desiree laughed, thrilled.

"And you will dance with Mademoiselle, Robert," Spigot said.

"You know he is a lost cause, Jeannot," Desiree chimed in before Robert had a chance to protest. "He does not dance the Charleston. He is too stiff," and she winked at Cristina. "Would you be a darling and stay by the piano? You can flip the pages for Max in my place, will you?"

Robert remained in the same place, placidly smoking his cigar, glad he would have one more chance to observe the lovely Cristina through half-closed eyelids.

"I am sorry if I did something to upset your wife. I didn't mean it," Cristina whispered to Max while he searched through the pages of music.

"Don't even give it another thought." He shook his head and looked up at her. "Old memories, just old memories. Not your fault, my dear," he said as he finished arranging the papers. Then louder, "C'mon, you wooden-legged *poilu*, I want to see how long you can dance before begging for mercy!"

Spigot's nose rose in the air to equal the height to which rose his pride, as it always did when he was challenged, and pulling himself to his mighty five feet three, turned to Desiree. He placed his right hand on her back and clasped her right hand with his left, holding it at shoulder height. He then turned to Max, an eyebrow raised in defiance, and waiting for the first tones, threw out the challenge: "Show me what you have, tommy!"

"Here we go," Max answered and started playing "The Charleston" from the prior year's Broadway musical *Runnin' Wild*.

One after another several Charleston songs filled the air. Desiree and Spigot seemed to have an everlasting amount of energy, their legs kicking back and forth, their elbows held high. Max, his bald head beaded with drops of perspiration from the effort of playing the piano, seemed to be having as much fun as the dancers. Cristina tapped her feet while turning the pages for Max, although he seemed to know most of the music by heart. She was happy to be able to witness the new fad—the Charleston—danced by people who seemed to know it well.

Max finished with George Botsford's energetic "Black and White Rag." The moment the music ended, Spigot bowed to Desiree and with a pirouette, collapsed into a chair and wiped his face with a handkerchief.

"What, already sounding retreat, Frog?" Robert mocked behind a cloud of smoke.

"The *poilu* is already beating retreat," Max claimed, provocatively. Spigot was too exhausted to respond, so he simply grimaced and waved the white handkerchief in a helpless gesture of surrender.

"Now, m'dear, you and I will dance, and I won't take no for an answer." Max stood up, took hold of Cristina's hand and, before she could protest, pulled her to the improvised dance floor.

Laughing and panting, Desiree had sunk to the piano stool. "Robbie darling, be a good boy and come here to give me a hand, don't be lazy." He attended to her call promptly, leaving behind his cigar and brandy. He bent low and said something in her ear. "I'll find something special that even you could dance to, don't you worry," she answered and started playing.

Max was not a great dancer, so he and Cristina danced apart. "She is a quick learner," he yelled to his wife between a twist and a kick, to Cristina's delight. When the first music ended, the mellow notes of "It Had to Be You" filled the air, and before Max could make a move, Robert had caught Cristina in his arms.

"My turn now, Maximilian. Go turn the pages for your wife, like a good boy." He then smiled down at Cristina's doe eyes.

As the music ended, another immediately started. Cristina warmed inwardly: Desiree had also found the sheet music for Ernesto Nazareth's "Eponina" among the others in the stack. Slowly and imperceptibly Robert guided their steps toward the stairs.

"It is too stuffy in here, don't you agree? Come upstairs with me." It was more a command than an invitation. "We can enjoy the sea breeze while we dance," and, without waiting for her agreement, he conducted her up the stairway.

She did not say anything but let herself be guided. The feeling was actually comforting. After her father's death, no other man had had a say in her life. She had to make all the decisions, and it was nice, for a change, to have someone she trusted take charge of things and tell her what to do—even if it was just choosing where to dance.

Up on the deck, most of the lights that were on when they arrived earlier were now off. A white half-moon shone down at them, imparting a milky gleam on their skin. His light eyes shimmered in the semi-darkness. For a moment he stood there, looking down, towering over her, and she felt such abandon that she feared she would have fallen had he not caught her hand in his firm grip. His left arm slipped behind her back and his palm felt the silky surface of her dress and yearned to discover the skin beneath it. Involuntarily her eyes closed, and she held to what was left of self-control to stop her head from bending backwards, offering her lips to him. She struggled to keep control of her legs, but as he started to dance, her body responded on an impulse she had not yet known. They moved smoothly, the soft cadence of the music channeled up the stairwell guiding his steps. She inhaled the scent of tobacco and shaving cologne that subtly emanated from him. The pressure of his arm on her back intensified slightly and she felt closer to his hard chest and through the contained strength of his hand holding hers, she could feel his pulse throb. Or was it hers?

As they glided around, the scenery shifted: first it was the lights along the Copacabana shore, like a long string of glimmering diamonds. Another slow turn showed the darkness beyond, sea and sky cast into one solid ebony wall; then there were the scattered lights of other boats against jagged mountains. Were they dancing, she wondered, the people in the other boats? The question floated in Cristina's mind like a feather on a gentle current of air. She felt Robert's breath, sweet and warm, on the side of her face. Did his lips just brush her hair? Slowly she leaned her head against his broad chest, and she felt it expand and contract as his lungs worked the night air—in and out. The music ended and another song began. Desiree's soft voice drifted up to them:

"'I love you, I love you, is all that I can say. I love you, I love you. The same old words I'm saying in the same old way.'"

When the music ended, Robert stopped moving. As if waking from a dream, she took a peek at his face. His eyes were closed and he remained silent, his jaw tight. She could not say how many seconds elapsed until his lids flickered and his eyes lowered to hers. His expression was serious, the look intense. She found herself unable to tear her gaze away from his. In his handsome face the strong jaw, the straight nose, and the perfect, dark eyebrows seemed to have been made to frame his well delineated lips. She saw them part, as if he was about to say something. He took a deeper breath that pushed his white shirt closer to her chin and made his nostrils move. Then his hands relaxed and, very slowly, he let go of her. He slightly turned and moved away, severing the immaterial thread that had held her spellbound. She stood there, her body faltering for a fraction of a second, as if suddenly fallen from a vacuum back into gravity's sway. Readjusting to the absence of his body, she walked passed him to the yacht's railing, more to find support than anything else.

Leaning against its cold surface, she let her eyes wander through the infinite darkness of an open sea she would not see even if the sun shone, so much her thoughts were concentrated, not on what was before her, but her feelings. The moonlight had carved strange scars on the water's surface. She heard sounds behind her and pictured him opening his cigarette case. Then it was the hiss of the lighter's flame and the sound of him inhaling the warm smoke. Why did her hands tremble, her stomach churn? Because she thought his eyes were upon her, was the answer. Beside her, suddenly his silhouette was delineated against the light emitted from the dining room downstairs. Music continued to play. His nearness effaced all musical sense from her and left a chaos of strange, unknown feelings in its place.

"This is a beautiful bracelet," he said looking pensively down at the golden chain clasped around her delicate wrist. "Black onyx, I believe."

"You might be correct," she agreed. "My mother says it is the color of my hair." She turned her wrist, watched as the electric light reflected on the stones. "It is an heirloom. I cannot remember not wearing it." She turned to face him. "My mother used to turn it twice around my wrist to be able to lock it because I insisted on wearing it," she laughed, looking back at it.

Robert knew where he had seen jewelry of the same style—necklace, earrings, and ring. Cristina's would be a perfect match for them.

"You do play beautifully."

She warmed to the sound of his low voice. It vibrated something inside her, like the cords on a harp played by gentle fingers. The background noise was like a world apart, distant and incoherent.

"Why did you choose to play that music?" The smoke he had just released lingered around his face creating a gauzy halo. His left hand rested on the balustrade so near she could have touched it if she so moved her little finger.

She shrugged her shoulders. "It chose me."

He turned a perplexed expression to her, but said nothing.

"You will laugh, but my hands simply started playing that music, just like that. It happens to me often," she explained

"How odd. That was my aunt's favorite music. She liked to play it for Desiree, you know, because of the color of her hair."

"Oh, what a nice coincidence," she said, pleased.

"Her mother died in very sad circumstances—she, her husband, and son."

Cristina's hand shot to her lips and her voice became a mere whisper. "Oh, I am so sorry. I didn't mean...I understand now why Desiree seemed so struck by the music."

"You couldn't possibly know." And as he looked at her, his eyes were a caress. He looked down into the water again and became pensive. A moment elapsed. "It was in 1915, they were travelling to England." Resting his hip against the railing he turned his body to face her, his eyes serious. "Have you heard of the *Lusitania*?"

Cristina nodded, her heart already heavy with the certainty of what was coming next.

"Well, they were on the ship—her mother, father, and brother. Their bodies were never found." After a brief silence, while he gazed at the darkness in the horizon, he continued: "Ricky had met this gal during the time he studied in England—Christina was her name." He turned and found her expressive eyes. "Desiree had not met her, but with her habit of giving nicknames to everyone, to her she was already Chris. They were coming back to the States, after his parents met her. Ricky was a wonderful fellow, adored by everyone. Desiree was very sick then and had stayed behind with us—my father and me." He took a deep breath, inhaling the cooling breeze, and shook his head. "Somehow she felt guilty for not dying with them. She found escape from her pain in alcohol and wild parties—and God only knows what else," he murmured as an afterthought. "I went to the war in '17, when we—when America—declared war, and when I came back, Max came with me." He smiled, remembering. "He wanted to meet Desiree, to help her. You see," he faced her again: "Christina was his sister. They both shared losses, you know." It seemed like it all had happened generations ago, he thought. "I don't know, but somehow he fell in love before even meeting Desiree. Well, Max accomplished what none of us was able to do: he rescued her. They married," he said softly, "and he has been her guardian angel since then. He adores her and lives for her. No children, unfortunately."

"I see," Cristina said in a low voice, mentally adding up the odd little things she noticed about Desiree that evening. "When I played that music, I reopened a wound," she murmured, dismayed. "Oh, how cruel! I am so sorry." She shut her eyes for a brief moment.

"Do not blame yourself. Her wound has never really healed. But, well, she must cope with memories no matter what, so don't feel bad. She has to look ahead, consider her future with a husband who adores her. And friends and family who love her." He gave her a smile and tossed the cigarette butt overboard.

Suddenly Max's voice was heard from the dining room, declaiming verses:

"'O compound of wrecked flesh, rent and torn asunder!'"

As Cristina turned to Robert, intrigued, other verses followed, as dramatically interpreted as those prior, and sometimes interrupted by Desiree's shrieking laugh: "'How do we e'er digest thy potency, I wonder. Cold, killed cattle pounded into paste!'"

And then Spigot took a turn, and in thickly French-accented English, he continued: "'Pressed into tins and shipped to us in haste. Greedily we eat thee, hot or cold or clammish!'"

As the recitation continued in the background, Cristina listened in amusement. Robert laughed as Max's words continued their reverberation from the dining room:

"'How welcomely thou thuddest in the mess tins of the famished. O leavings of a jackal's feast! O carrion sublime!'"

"'No matter how we scoff at thee, we eat thee every time. Ah, corned willie.'" The last verse had been shouted with passion in a duet, the last syllable stretched as much as their breath could carry it. Explosions of laughter followed.

"This is a joke from the war, about the corned beef the American troops ate," Robert explained and they laughed for a while. Folding his arms on his chest, he considered her. "I think my friends went over the edge with the rams," he said and winked an eye. She gave him a perplexed look. "I am sorry. You speak English so well that I forget it is not your mother tongue. I meant to say that they seem to be drunk—actually too drunk," he explained. "Now what about you?" He tilted his head to one side, changing the subject. "What do you expect of the future? You are very young. You certainly have plans."

The question took her by surprise. It would have been simple to explain that the lack of time while caring for her father, then later the lack of money were the cause of her abandoning her dreamed career as a classical pianist. But that would make her sound like a complainer. Besides, what would a man like him, who came from a wealthy background, know about lack of money? She shook her head involuntarily, distractedly stroking the bracelet on her wrist. "Oh, I don't expect a lot. I actually don't have much time to think of the future lately. I am very busy working," she said and tried to smile.

He detected melancholy in her tone and realized his question was not fair, nor had he the right to interrogate her—especially when he already knew so much about her rather precarious situation. It had not been a fair question, and he chided himself for having asked.

"Look, a falling star," she exclaimed, pointing at the dark sky above their heads.

"Make a wish, quick, for both of us," he teased her.

She shook her head, her mouth set in a sad line, her eyes scrutinizing the sky. "During hot summer nights, my father and I used to go to the roof of our house to watch the sky," she started slowly. "Every time he saw a falling star, he asked me to make a wish...for both of us. I no longer dare to make wishes." She looked at him and the sadness in her eyes awoke something inside him.

"Do you miss him very much?" he asked quietly.

"Yes," she answered simply.

His fingers took hold of her chin, and on her upturned face he saw tears well in her eyes. She did not recoil as his face approached hers. Her eyes showed no surprise—as there is none as night succeeds day.

Fascinated by the dark pools behind the long, curled lashes, he made the wait longer, extending her anticipation but also spurring the desire he had felt since he had first seen her. As his lips touched hers, she closed her eyes and a low sigh escaped her. The sound came to her as distant, from somewhere outside herself. She could not think straight; she could not ask what was happening. She could only let go, her body soft and warm as a cup of hot chocolate—yes, like the hot chocolate Maria made for her on cold nights. The thought crossed her mind like lightening cutting through fluffy clouds. She almost laughed at the absurdity of it! Her hands shyly slid up to the back of his neck, her fingers searching the softness of his hair. Enveloped in his arms, the proximity of his strong body against hers, so close as if they were one, her mind cleared of all thought and she plunged into the unknown feelings without fear. His mouth rested longer against hers, his body concealed hers inside his embrace. As a groan escaped his chest, she felt suddenly awakened and was startled by the silence that surrounded them.

Silence. Suddenly, understanding sank in: they were alone. And they were kissing. Oh, Lord! As her arms disengaged his neck, she propelled her body away from his so quickly that she had to prop herself against the balustrade to keep from falling to her weakened knees. He lingered above her, his arms at his sides, eyes opened, while slowly her refusal dawned on him, and one word from her sobered his desire.

"No!" Her voice sounded hoarse, thick with the feelings she had to suffocate. She smoothed her dress, her eyelids lowered to avoid what she saw reflected in his face.

"I am sorry," he rubbed his forehead, his thoughts trying to take control over his feelings. What was he thinking? "I didn't mean to . . . ."

"It is late," she said hastily, keeping her eyes down, trying to ignore her throbbing chest. "We are alone, the others seem to have retired, and…and it is not… appropriate," she stammered, continuing to avoid his eyes; the fear of what she'd read in them acted like a sobering tonic. "Please, take me home."

"Yes, of course." He wet his lips nervously, trying to put some order to his tumultuous thoughts. He hesitated a few seconds then offered an arm, which she chose not to see but followed him down to the same launch that had earlier carried them to the yacht. The hand he had taken to help her into the launch was now quickly withheld. What happened back there, he asked himself, upset for allowing his feeling to take control. He had never lost control like that. He felt he had taken advantage of her youth and inexperience and now did not quite know what to tell her, how to apologize. He had acted like an irresponsible adolescent. Damn you, you idiot, he chastised himself.

It was a quick and silent trip. They found the cab dutifully waiting. She did not want to, but he insisted and took her home, riding in the front seat. No words were exchanged, and the driver kept any comments about the lovely night to himself. When the car stopped in front of her house, he walked her to the door and tried to explain himself.

"Please believe me when I tell you it is not my habit to lure young ladies to some quiet spot and try to seduce them," he pleaded, half serious, half joking.

"It is as much my fault as it is yours," was her surprising answer. "You certainly felt you could…take me in your arms because…well…it is clear that I somehow signaled the permission…" She felt gauche and avoided his eyes.

"No, no," he eagerly assured her. "That is not how it happened! You trusted me to be a gentleman, and I abused your trust."

"I am really tired, Mr. Laughton," she said wearily. She turned the key in the lock. Oh, how much she wanted that night to end…and yet not. "Good night," she said in a voice she willed to calmness, and quietly shut the door.

\* \* \*

Through his opera glasses, Daniel had seen when the usher approached Cristina and handed her a piece of paper. He followed the usher's gesture and saw Robert wave at her from his box. He imagined the girl blushing in excitement as she hurriedly tucked the paper into her purse and followed the usher. That made him feel sick, and the more he watched her, the angrier he became. From that moment on, he paid little attention to the music, his whole being focused on the box where Cristina sat, her face turned to the stage. He could see the American right behind her.

At the end of the presentation, on the way out, she did not see Daniel in the crowd as he followed her down the steps, yet he was so close behind he could have touched her if he but stretched out his arm. He captured the glances she exchanged with the American, the smiles, and a feeling of revolt at his impotency overwhelmed him. The marble rail of the stairway ended at a beautiful female face made of copper that rested on a scroll pedestal. He leaned his head against its cool surface for a few seconds but found no remedy for the fire that burned inside him.

Forgotten was the feeling of awe he always experienced while within the majestic building—twin soul of the Opéra in Paris. In its place something different emerged, so much stronger that it hid the surrounding splendor. The wide, squared Corinthian columns of polished marble that opened to the bifurcated stairway and held the foyer; the vaulted frescoed ceilings and walls painted by Rodolfo Amoedo and Eliseu Visconti; the beautiful sculptures chiseled by Rodolfo Bernardelli; the clusters of gleaming electric lights hanging on the walls or gathered by sculptures of bronze nymphs—all lost their appeal to him.

Hate, frustration, and envy escorted him outside the building as in a nightmare. One foot, than another, he was pushed forward by the crowd in a sea of confusing sounds, movements, and colors. Outside, his cheeks felt moist and he looked up, but the crescent moon shone in a cloudless sky pregnant with gleaming stars. These little droplets that blurred his vision, trickled down his face, and left a moist path behind them had come not from the nightly sky.

His throat was dry as straw and he felt a desperate need to quench the thirst that tortured him. He suddenly recollected the conversation he'd had earlier with the waiter at Confeitaria Colombo, about Ramires, the private investigator. On an impulse he veered in the direction of the so-called *Braço de Ferro*—the Bar Adolph. Perhaps luck would be with him and he might meet this

Ramires there. He didn't have a plan. He only felt he had to keep moving, and his legs carried him first through the wide cosmopolitan streets, and then he was immersed in the darker streets, the remains of the old downtown.

His brain slowly unclouded. He realized that by contacting the private investigator, he might be able to obtain information about the American, and depending on what that information was, he could use as it a weapon against him. Who knows, it might be something so bad that he could use it to separate him from Cristina.

While he walked he considered the best way to approach Ramires and concluded that direct approach might put the man on guard. If Daniel were to get him to open up, it had to look as if it had been a chance meeting. He needed to find a way to approach and befriend this Ramires. Simple plans were always best, he thought. And as he turned the corner of the Assembléia Street, he saw the sign atop a wide door: Bar Adolph—the "Iron Arm" that the waiter at Colombo had mentioned.

It was still early. A couple of more respectable clients who probably worked late that day quietly drank their beer while reading newspapers that looked the worse for much handling. These clients would be heading home soon for an also quiet and respectable dinner and a relaxing weekend. A small gathering of men sat at a table littered with glasses, playing cards, their cigarettes hanging low on tense lips, and sleeves rolled up. On the table nearer to the door a young woman sat alone, her short, bottle-blond hair spilling out of an electric-purple cloche hat. It matched a satin dress that did not exactly bury her light under a bushel. She stole an appraising look at Daniel. To his embarrassment—and delight—she leaned on her elbows and offered the generous sight of creamy cleavage. It was not common to see a real gentleman in the neighborhood, she thought, so one must take all possible advantage of such an auspicious event. A bit on the smallish side, but he still seemed to be a gentleman, she concluded.

He found a table facing the door and sat down. With a nervous finger he tried to loosen the neck of his shirt and let some air cool the sudden warmth he felt at the girl's inspection of him. Clearing his throat he pushed up his glasses that had slipped down the bridge of his damp nose. He called the waiter and ordered a cold beer and some meatballs.

"O, Rafael, a sweaty blond for the gentleman here," the waiter shouted at the top of his lungs as he approached a man behind the counter, "and fry me some meatballs, will ya?"

The blond gave Daniel a wide smile and, petting her bobbed hair, winked at him. As he risked a few quick peeks at her, she kept smiling. When she finally got a shy smile in response to her advances, she rose and directed her steps to his table. The silence was sudden. All male eyes were upon her, including Daniel's, mesmerized. She sashayed, and the sway of her round hips against the silky dress told a sensuous tale. Fascinated, Daniel watched as she came to a stop right in front of him, her eyes boldly on his. He took a loud gulp. His face turned slowly a deep shade of red; the flush spread over his forehead, over his ears and even down his neck.

"Name is Dulce." Her voice was low and smooth. Her hand was presented to him in a way she considered glamorous: at the end of an outstretched arm, the tips of her delicate fingers hinting at the mildest of touches.

Daniel quickly stood up and gingerly took the limp fingers. He then held a chair and awkwardly motioned her to it.

"Da-Daniel," he stuttered as she sat down.

Through one slit in the skirt, a bit of a black garter made a grand appearance and revealed the beginning of a round, creamy thigh as she sat facing him and crossed her legs. She opened a tiny purse and pulled a pack of cigarettes and matches from it. Her movements were slow and deliberate and her seductive eyes kept going back to his. She seemed to be very young, and even with her face heavily made up, the freshness of her skin was evident. Her thin eyebrows were tamed on a descending arch, giving her the melancholy air of a Pola Negri, the Polish actress and singer. Her mouth had been redesigned with red lipstick to mimic the geisha lips, so in vogue.

Around them the place resumed its normal hum.

"May I?" she asked, pulling one cigarette from the pack.

"Su-sure," he stuttered, his distaste for cigarette smoke having magically vanished.

As she motioned the cigarette case to him, he thanked her with a shy smile. She waited until he realized it and lit her cigarette. She thanked him and fluttered her blackened eyelids.

"That means sweet in Latin. I-I mean," he stammered at her puzzled look, "your name, it means…sweet. In Latin," he ended lamely

"And there is no one sweeter than Dulce, darling," she said and grinned provocatively.

"Please," he offered, as he noticed that her eyes were attracted to the round golden delicacies in the dish that had just landed on the table. And as she eagerly ate, he asked, "Could I, er, offer you something else to eat?"

"Oh, how kind of you! That would be swell."

\* \* \*

Dulce chewed the last of the hors d'oeuvre. She had spoken little while eating since all her senses seemed to have been concentrated on the act of chewing and ingesting more food until the bitter end. A deep sigh and a contented smile were Daniel's reward. Then she pushed the dish away and, sucking her teeth, got hold of a toothpick. Embarrassed, Daniel looked away.

"Down on my uppers lately," she said when her dental hygiene was finished. "Short of money," she elaborated.

At that very moment a tall man entered the bar. He looked around and his eyes narrowed as they focused on Dulce. Then he saw Daniel. Now, that daisy sitting with the sheba—he mulled— where had he seen that map before? Then he remembered he had seen him with the American's girl, Cristina. What the hell was he doing with Dulce, he asked himself, annoyed.

Of course he was far from claiming ownership, but with all the dough he had come by that day, sure enough he and Dulce would soon find some understanding. He beamed inwardly at the thought, and approached the table. He was certainly not dizzy over Dulce, but, boy, was she a looker!

All the while Daniel, recalling the conversation he had had with the waiter at Colombo, concluded that this was none other than Ramires. The one with the long…how had the waiter described the investigator? Long map—yes, that was it. Equine, he thought, the face was definitely equine. And as these things occurred to Daniel, the man appeared beside him, and he could not help blushing as though his thoughts could have been read.

"Dulce," Ramires addressed her after a long, scrutinizing glance at Daniel.

"Well, look at ya," she smiled broadly, examining him from top to bottom. "You are mighty spiffy in those new rags, Ramires."

"You think so?" He grinned and passed a hand over his carefully pomaded hair, while inspecting her with hungry eyes. "You don't look too shabby yourself, Dulce." He pulled the chair beside her and sat down, ignoring Daniel.

"What's it gonna be, Ramires," the waiter standing beside him asked. "Beer?"

"For all of us." Meanwhile he deliberately pulled an overfilled wallet out of his jacket and smirked as Dulce's wide eyes assessed its contents. "Or whatever the gentleman here is having," he added, quickly scanning the table.

"Oh, no, thank you, just water for me, please," Daniel answered nervously and found three pairs of scandalized eyes staring at him. He had been sitting quietly, divided between joy at this chance encounter, and discomfort at the novelty the situation presented.

"Water? C'mon, pal, dip the bill," Ramires exclaimed, in what was an indecipherable comment to Daniel. "Just one," he insisted. And, not waiting for an answer, Ramires turned to the waiter: "Beer it will be—and bring us something to eat, too. The usual." He then turned a scrutinizing gaze to Daniel and, extending him a large, bony paw as the waiter left, introduced himself rather informally: "Ramires."

"My pleasure. Daniel Cabral," and he inadvertently winced at the man's strong handshake.

"C'mon, tell me how you got a hold of all that spinach, Ramires," Dulce enquired, laying an enticing hand on his shoulder.

"Got paid today, babe." And seeing her raised eyebrow, added: "What? D'you think I stole it or something? I'm a working man! This American client has the bees, and I got some of it right here," he bragged, patting his pocket, and gave a hearty laugh.

Daniel rightfully concluded that the American in question was Robert but was at a loss to how he would get any information from Ramires. Worse, he didn't even know what he was looking for. But the opportunity soon arose. After his third beer, the man was more talkative and friendly, while Dulce was content to just listen. He detailed Robert's case, names and all, without any prompting. He then started enumerating other cases he professed having solved, but Daniel's mind was concentrated on the story he had just heard concerning Robert. He carefully committed the details to memory. He was certain what he had gathered could be used to his advantage; he just needed time and quiet to think up a plan and put all that knowledge to use. His thoughts were disturbed by Dulce's voice.

"Excuse me, gentlemen," she said while she disentangled her waist from Ramires' grip. "I gotta go see the john," she giggled.

As she stood up, Daniel sprang to his feet, to Dulce's and Ramires' surprise. As the girl walked away, Ramires noisily dragged his chair near Daniel's.

"Pipe that, fella." Drawing his face near to Daniel's, and wagging an uncertain finger, he continued: "If you're interested, think twice, 'cause I was first," he said in a thick voice, the fricatives demanding more energy to be formed.

Trying to avoid the man's breath, saturated with the aroma of alcohol and pickled onions, Daniel looked mystified at Ramires's words.

"Listen here, I am talking about the jane!"

"Oh," Daniel smiled in understanding. "I have *no* interest in her," he said with a dismissive wave of his hand. And as Ramires raised one of his bushy eyebrows in perplexity, Daniel continued: "I mean, she is pretty and…and…nice and all that, but…but I can see you two already knew each other. Besides she seems to have a marked inclination for you. I…I never meant to intrude—."

"That's quite alright. We understand each other then, and that's what matters," he said, relaxing, and his large paw massaged Daniel's frail shoulder. "So, I guess it's time for you to breeze off then," and he motioned at the door with his head. "If you need a blower to call a hack, it's behind the counter. They'll let you use it." And as the other man hesitated, mystified, he growled in a low voice: "Sneak, pal."

Daniel felt more than he understood that he was being told

to phone for a taxi if he needed one. He patted himself on the back for the ease with which he quickly extricated himself from Ramires's clutches—and Dulce's. His mind was like a whirlpool, excitedly wondering what to do with the portentous news that had fallen into his lap. After being surrounded with so much alcoholic vapors, he was in need of fresh air in order to sort out the information and conceive a plan. He bowed a bit unsteadily and took his leave just before Dulce got back to the table.

"Where's my friend?" she asked. Her eyes narrowed: "Did you scare him away, Ramires?"

"Your *friend* had to leave, Dulce. Now it's just you and me, babe," and saying so he pulled her down to the chair near him.

* * *

On his way back to the yacht, after he saw Cristina to her door, Robert pondered on that night's events. Why the hell did he even care whether he had upset her or not? Tomorrow he would have forgotten her for sure, so why did her opinion of him matter at all? It had just been a kiss, for crying out loud. Besides, he was sure she had also enjoyed it, he argued inwardly. Yet he knew that kiss had meant a lot to a girl like Cristina—and also to him, if he were truthful with himself.

He had promised to help his father. Well, he had helped and the job was done. Then why the hell didn't he telegraph an outline of the final report gathered by the private investigator to his father and let *him* deal with it? That's what he gained for bringing Desiree along and allowing her to mingle in his business. But, no, he had to be fair: Desiree had done nothing—surprisingly— considering her penchant for match-making. He had precipitated the events by following Cristina all over town—unnecessarily, by the way—like a complete idiot. As if that were not enough, he invited her to join his party in the theater. And just by observing her, he could easily conclude she was not the kind of girl who gave herself to the first man who sought her.

This time he realized something different was happening. With Cristina it was not the matter of a comfortable, disposable mock-relationship. Then why had he even approached the girl in the first place? No, he rebelled against his own feelings; he was not ready, not yet. Well, maybe…some day, in the future. But…heck, since when had he started thinking even of the possibility of . . . . He shook his head completely dismissing this train of thought from his mind. He'd better start watching out. But he could not help thinking that there was something different about her. She got him to tell about Desiree, their childhood, and all without asking a single question. What next? He would be confessing his love life to her over tea! He laughed aloud at the thought. Now that would not be a subject to be discussed with a young lady of good family. But seriously, he had always thought himself immune to…well, these kinds of thoughts and feelings heard so much in love songs. And here he was, acting like an idiotic, lovesick schoolboy.

Robert tied off the launch and boarded the yacht. At the thought of going to his stuffy bedroom, he decided to enjoy the cooler breeze on the deck for a little longer. He dropped onto a stretcher and, taking a deep breath of the night air, laid back. The lights were out and the darkness was soothing. The sky was sprinkled with stars and he recalled similar nights spent in a *dahabeah*—an Egyptian passenger boat—watching the stars and lulled to sleep by the Nile water lap at the hull. The difference was that the heat was humid in Brazil, while in Cairo it was drier. He remembered the cheap Egyptian cigarettes he liked to smoke while there. He had to make sure Spigot sneaked some out for him on his next visit to Cairo. He clasped both hands behind his neck and felt the nightly breeze caress his face. With eyes closed he concentrated on the sounds around him: the murmur of the water against the hull of the boat; the stretched cables thumping against poles; the gentle creaking of wood and metal; his deepened, cadenced breathing...

\* \* \*

Light was fighting the darkness—and winning—brushing the sky with gashes of purple, then pink and red, and then pure blue slowly began to take over, speckled with a few gauzy clouds. Robert opened his eyes and realized he had fallen asleep on the deck still dressed in his formal wear. Sitting up he took a deep breath of the delicious morning air. He stretched his arms and, yawning mightily, gave his hair an energetic tousling. As the events of the prior night came back to him, he tried to make sense of them, and failed. But at the thought of Cristina's rosy lips, his heart started beating like a drum. Heck, no, he thought, rubbing his face vigorously, I'm not going to fall for those thoughts again. Perhaps some action would help stop his thinking? Well, he must find something to at least distract him. Swimming—yes, that would help. Besides, his body needed exercise. Yet deep inside he was aware that lack of exercise was not the cause of his mental fidgeting, but the cool sea water would at least help clear his mind. He stood up with a decided movement and went down to his cabin to change.

* * *

It was all in vain: as his arms tired with the effort of swimming, his mind incessantly analyzed the same thoughts he had entertained before falling asleep the night before. Overwhelmed and frustrated, he stopped swimming. In a cathartic attempt to break through the regularity of his thoughts, he hit the water with clenched fists. But the only thing he got was flying drops of blinding salty water that smarted his eyes. He licked the droplets from his lips and wiped them off his eyelashes. Then he broke up in laughter at his silly behavior. There had been many women in his life; he no longer remembered their names, not even their faces. But this mere girl had suddenly landed in his life and disturbed the balance he had long enjoyed. He could not understand what had bitten him.

Robert had spoken with Cristina just a few times, yet the thought of her was constantly with him. He opened to her like a clam in boiling water; he ran after her all over Rio, covertly watching her every movement; he went to her store with the lame excuse of buying music—when he could not play even a child's harmonica; he lured her to join his party; he kissed her the first time she was alone with him; and here he was, clearly trying to reason how this might be *her* fault! He could not contend that she had done anything to lure or attract him.

He smiled at the recollection of the angry Cristina marching towards him at Colombo, her beautiful face with such a forbidding expression. If only she knew how adorable she looked.

He smiled at the recollection of her dismayed countenance when he countered her charge that he was following her. But he must admit: guilty as charged. He was the one following her. She had turned embarrassed eyes to him–two lovely pools of dark, deep water—and he had succumbed to their unintended charm. She was no longer the marching soldier on a mission, but had offered him the most delicious smile, the *coup de grâce* to his heart. They had talked about trivial subjects, he could not remember exactly what. It did not matter. The thing was that she had made him feel as though they had known each other for ages. Her company was both amusing and relaxing.

A few screaming seagulls hovering above his head called him back to the present. Forcibly recalled to the world outside, he decided it was time to return to the yacht. Definitely he had to occupy his mind to stop thinking nonsense. Maybe it would be best if he finished his business soon and just went back home. The bustle of New York might be the cure for these foolish thoughts. With this in mind he paddled on his back until he reached the steps of the yacht. But by then the decision to go back home had evanesced like the wisps of clouds he had seen in the sky when he woke up.

"Did you have a good exercise?" Bunky, Robert's valet cum guardian, asked, handing him a white plush bathrobe. He was more solicitous than usual, overwhelmed by guilt at falling asleep and—shame of all shames—unaware that Robert had spent the night on the deck.

"Yes, thank you, Bunky." And he could not help smiling. It was funny to watch the huge bulk of a man wear a meek expression on his generally forbidding face. "I am going down for a quick shower, and then I would like to have some coffee and breakfast. The usual: bacon and eggs. Can you see to that? And, please, ask Eugênio to see me before he leaves for the market."

As he walked on the deck he saw Desiree and stopped to talk with her. "What, already up?" He mocked a jaw-dropping expression. "Do my eyes deceive me?" Accordingly he rubbed his eyes, and, walking to where she was, sat in the neighboring chair with a content sigh. He picked up a book she had laid down at his approach and read out loud: "The Cat's Eye, R. Austin Freeman." And turning to her: "A new mystery book, I see."

She yanked the book from his hand and threw him an annoyed glance. "Dr. Thorndyke, my favorite mystery book character, if you care to know! Although," she pursed her lips, tilted her head to one side, and pondered the subject: "I love Sayer's Lord Peter. And Dr. Fu-Manchu. Oh, and loved that David Carroll detective from Octavus Cohen." Then her mind returned to the reason for her annoyed demeanor: "Anyway, you are the cause of my early rise. Yes, *you*," she insisted, seeing as he was startled at her words. "This morning—if one can call five o'clock morning—when your overgrown body fell into the water and a gigantic wave hit this bathtub, it woke me up." He looked at her with an apologetic expression. "The fact that you jumped from right above my bedroom window is obviously of no consequence, of course, had this nutshell been a real yacht." She waived her hand in a dismissive gesture at her surroundings. "And since I could no longer sleep, well, I thought to myself, why not go to the deck and enjoy the excruciatingly humid morning breeze *you* seem to love. And here I am," she pushed her glasses up her nose and laid back on the chair, closing her eyes. "So, had fun swimming your twenty-mile marathon? And that was just chit-chat: I don't really care to know."

He said in a meditative tone: "You know, you should try some physical exercise. It would do you good," and gave the tip of her nose a light squeeze. "Now what *really* is the problem? What's amiss?

As he seemed to always know when something troubled her, she decided to go for the jugular: "Why did you have to hire one of...*them*?"

Robert looked at her puzzled. "Them? Could you be a bit more specific?"

"Last night I did not miss his last name: Kneip..."

Robert took a deep breath and shook his head despondently as he realized Desiree was referring to the new cook. "Desiree," he replied with a touch of asperity, "Eugênio is not even really German, he never went to Germany, nor does he speak the language. He's merely a German descendant. Can't you accept the fact that the war is over? Besides, not all Germans are bad." And he immediately regretted having spoken harshly. But, heck, she would have to put this story behind her, eventually. The war *was* over and she had to accept that the world continued turning and nations—people—went about their business. "Just leave the man alone, will you? Let him do his job," he pleaded, upset with the turn the conversation had taken.

She bit her lower lip and turned her head from him. "So we got over the idea that a good German is a dead German, all right," she chuckled bitterly.

Silly girl. He knew she would come to grips with her ghosts, but it was taking an awfully long time, and he was starting to despair. He would have to talk to Max and see if anything could be done.

"Well, I guess I will have to live with the fact the Krauts murdered my entire family, then things turned and now they're everybody's darlings. I just hope this one doesn't poison our food." But before he could say anything, she abruptly changed the subject—a strategy she largely utilized to end a conversation that had become uncomfortable to then start an even more uncomfortable one. "So, how was it last night with Cris? You two seemed to be having a jolly time. You even danced with her–cheek to cheek, imagine that! Extra, extra, read all about it: Robert Laughton, for whom all the flappers in Manhattan sigh, spotted dancing cheek to cheek on the deck of his father's yacht, having only the moon for witness. Oh, how romantic…" She sighed deeply and holding her hands together, nested them against her breast, blinking her lashes at him.

"Desiree, I must stop you before you go further with this nonsense." He was able to control his voice and keep it level. The last thing he wanted was for this scatterbrained creature to have an inkling of how on the mark her comments were. "She does not strike me as someone who would be content to have a passing affair and then be left behind," he said.

A wide, candid smile parted Desiree's lips as she sat up and continued: "But there you go, you got my point! Yes, yes, and—yes. It has never crossed my mind that you should have a passing affair with Cris."

He closed his eyes, giving himself time to resist the urge to wring her little neck with both hands. He opened them to see a suspiciously innocent expression in hers: "Desiree, what are you planning in that little scheming head of yours?"

"Oh, well, if you really want to know–and I guess you will learn it sooner or later," she said and brought her face closer to his, confidentially, and taking hold of one of his hands continued, "I really think–oh, and Max agrees with me, by the way—that you should marry her."

For a few seconds he was wordless, but he quickly recovered the power of speech. "Me? Marry?" He yanked his hand free, no longer able to hide his irritation.

"Yes. You. Marry. And why not, pray tell me?" she asked with wide opened, childish eyes.

He searched his brain for an answer, but, for once, it was at a loss for a smart retort. "Well…Why *yes*, I ask you?"

All the while Desiree watched him carefully. Her scrutinizing expression, her twitching lips that barely hid a smile, suddenly irritated him more than any prank she had ever played on him since they were kids.

"You should get out of the sun, cousin. I think it's fried your brain." Retaining his calm at great cost, he stood up, holding back the urge to just break into a run. With steady hands he tightened the knot in his robe's sash, with a bit too much strength, and left, hoping she had not noticed. But he knew from experience that that short exchange would only exacerbate Desiree's matchmaking nature, and no doubt more was to come.

Desiree adjusted the pillow behind her neck and, pushing the sun spectacles up the bridge of her nose, laid back. Robert's reaction confirmed her suspicion. This time, she was sure, her cousin was caught. And she was going to make sure he would not escape.

As Robert walked away, her limpid mezzo-soprano voice joyfully raised in a provocative interpretation of Cherubino's aria: "Voi, che sapete che cosa è amor. Donne, vedete, s'io l'ho nel cor, Donne, vedete, s'io l'ho nel cor, Donne, vedete, s'io l'ho nel cor." He gritted his teeth hard, but kept a sedate pace down the steps to his cabin.

Extremely satisfied with her teasing, Desiree resumed enjoying the warmth of the morning. It was still relatively cool, so she decided to remain a few more minutes and enjoy it. Suddenly she burst out laughing, surprising the men working on the deck. She always loved teasing Robert. The only way to learn how he felt was to upset him so much he would be caught off guard. Desiree knew well his calm countenance of a few moments ago was mere show and only confirmed what she knew: the little Brazilian had reached into his heart. Well, nature would certainly do the rest. But if it did not, she would find a way to give it a little push, just to be sure of the outcome.

# CHAPTER 5

In Copacabana Cristina opened her bedroom window and took a deep breath of morning air. In the backyard birds chirped and flew to and fro in the branches of the papaya trees outside her window. The rays of the early sun through its foliage imprinted brilliant spots everywhere, a veritable lace made of light and shade. Tiny drops of dew clung to leaves, budding fruits, and petals, and sparkled as the light touched them, like tiny diamonds the night had lavished on them.

Just beyond, other small trees were garlanded with buds, promises of fruits that would enchant her lazy weekend afternoons. Soon peaches, plums, limes, and apples would infuse the warm air turning the miniature orchard into a magic stretch of greens, reds, yellows and purples. Even from where she stood on the second floor, she felt the scent of the clusters of rosemary and lavender that lined the garden paths. Honeysuckle entwined through the lattice on the wall outside her window carried up a subtle perfume. She rested her elbows on the windowsill, nesting her face on her cupped hands and couldn't help smiling back at the day's alacrity. The beauty of the morning had turned the prior night's guilty thoughts into a distant fog.

And as she considered the events that marked the end of the prior night, she concluded that, in fact, she had not done anything wrong. It had been a mere brush of lips–and a shudder of pleasure shot through her body. She closed her eyes and thought of the men she knew–her father, Daniel, her colleagues at the Music Institute.

Robert was different from all of them. But that was not quite it. At his proximity she experienced mixed and conflicting feelings. She felt anxious, nervous, and even tongue-tied. But, contradictorily, also relaxed, comfortable. Yes, it was not so much that he was different from all the men she knew. It was that he made her *feel* different. A knock on the door, then Maria's pleasant face peeped inside.

"You up already? I thought I heard your window open." Her voice was as merry as her face. "Coffee's ready. And guess what?" she asked, her eyes widening. "I made that corn bread you love. Just got it out of the oven. C'mon and eat it while it's warm. What a nice day, isn't it?" she added, before disappearing.

"I will be there in a minute," Cristina called in response.

She let her body slip into bed again and the imagery that filled her mental retina was peopled by one tall, blond man. "Robert," she whispered softly. The name had an unfamiliar taste but sounded so good that she repeated it gain. Robert... A warm feeling slowly spread through her body. Ashamed at her inappropriate thoughts, she chided herself mentally. This man— she started a speech directed to her conscience—is certainly used to women falling on him like bees on honey! And that is how he sees you, Cristina, you're just another bee—and a tiny, unimportant one at that. She thought the comparison was worthy of a cheap melodrama and laughed. Next she tried hard to shame herself for having lost control so easily the night before in the yacht; in the same breath and quite incoherently, she also blamed Robert for what happened. But deep inside she knew the only thing he had done was to merely look into her eyes. Yes, and her knees wobbled, her heart jumped to her throat, her tongue tied, and inside her that fast working of heart and veins took her breath away. So the verdict at which her conscience finally arrived acquitted both defendants.

She eyed the clock; it already marked six thirty. No reason fighting against it, so she sprang out of bed, the last fragments of the night's events scattered by her hurried movements. She reached for her housecoat and went out the door to the kitchen for a quick breakfast while Maria changed.

The best thing to do was to stay away from Robert, she primly concluded while slicing a large chunk of cornbread and mixing two spoons of sugar in the cup, full to the rim with fragrant coffee. Yet deep inside she knew it was a plan easier conceived than executed. She sighed in deep frustration and shrugged. What was a girl to do?

\* \* \*

Robert repressed a yawn. He had slept on the deck in his clothes and was awake at the first morning light. Then, like a stupid teenage boy (he would not dare adding *in love*), he had followed Eugênio to an open market, and for what? For the chance of sneaking a view of that frail little thing! Besides it being a childish whim, following Cristina in an open market was not part of what his father had sent him to do. The thought did not have a chance to mature as he killed it in the cradle: he was actually in the market to accompany Eugênio, and that was all. And he found a comforting excuse in the memory of the many times he had joined Manny, his father's cook, on his visits to the market in New York.

As he walked through the open market, Robert was besieged by its many scents and colors. They enveloped him and it was hard to remain untouched. He had been in open markets in Egypt, but this one was different. It was cleaner and the air did not exude any fetid scent—most certainly due to its temporary character: a section of a street housed the market, which was later cleaned and reopened in the afternoon. Also, the women here did not cover their hair and faces with veils. Yet, like there, the merchants' calls filled the air, like swords crossing blades but never touching: you were called to at every stall by strident voices.

Here a merchant announced delicious apples—*"Maçãs deliciosas!"* There another praised the virtues of his papayas, good for the stomach and the heart—*"Mamão, bom prô estômago e prô coração!"* Ahead a couple of men sang the praises of the fish they sold: the best, and fresh from the sea—*"Peixes, fresquinhos, recém saídos do mar!"* It was funny the way these Brazilians pronounced the "s" as *"sh"*—which was very much how the Portuguese did. His new cook, Eugênio, who was from the southern part of Brazil, pronounced it differently though.

His attention was taken by a curvaceous mulatta with almond eyes as green as pools. She opened a wide smile that unveiled the whitest teeth he had ever seen and tried to sell him a melon. She held to him a bright rosy slice of fruit, and fluttering a pair of long eyelashes, asked if the handsome young man would like to try it—"*Moço bonito, quer um pedaço de melão?*" He smiled and, accepting the offer, gestured to Eugênio to pay her and get the melon. Way too many temptations in this kind of market, he thought. He shook his head, amused, and sank his teeth in the meet of the juicy fruit.

"You can't buy everything that is offered to you, Sir," Eugênio admonished him.

"Eugênio, you wanted me to refuse an offer coming from such hands?" he asked jokingly. "Now, enlighten me on open market etiquette."

"If you allow me, Sir, it would be best if you just follow me and let me do the buying—and the talking. We are both too foreign-looking already, and if this crowd figures out you are indeed a foreigner, prices will rise higher than the Statue of Liberty."

So Robert obediently fell to the background. Suddenly, far ahead, he saw Cristina, distracted with her purchases. He chose to remain in obscurity, observing her from a safe distance. She looked fresh and bright in the morning sun. A large straw hat sheltered her to the shoulders from the morning sun. Her happy face made her look more like a child choosing her toys. Her hands touched the colorful fruits, and she brought them near her nose, inhaling their sweet scent. Like a nymph she meandered around the stalls, and with Maria's help deposited the choices in a large wicker basket they both carried. As they walked to the next stall, a stout young man solicitously came from behind his counter, his face beaming with contentment.

"Miss Cristina," he greeted her with a thick Portuguese accent. "Here, I have something made especially for you by my mother, a delicacy from our beloved Azores," and he delivered a small parcel into her hands while casting loving eyes at her.

"Joaquim," she said and smiled at him prettily, "you shouldn't do that. Your mother is spoiling me." She graciously accepted the gift and thanked him. She had heard him praise it so much—*Cornucópias*, as they are called in the Azores—and was happy to be honored with a sample. She speculated to what lengths

Joaquim had to go to steal these from his grumpy mamma. The few occasions when she had the chance to meet his mother in the market, the portly Mrs. Taveira had made abundantly clear she did not approve of her son's visible penchant for Cristina.

"Just a small nothing," Joaquim said and made a dismissive gesture, but his face expressed the delight he took in pleasing Cristina. "Just make sure you hold them carefully; they are very frail."

"How awfully kind of your mother, Joaquim," Maria teased him, smiling inwardly. "Her liking for Cristina is such it always amazes me. The kind lady!"

Cristina covertly elbowed Maria and stopped her antics. The poor man reddened and stammered his speech to reassure Cristina of his mother's fondness for her, while he packed her purchases. They thanked him and, as they walked away, almost ran into Eugênio.

"Miss Cristina," he greeted her and slightly bowed to Maria.

Cristina instinctively searched for Robert, which was not lost on Eugênio. He turned to the direction he expected to find him, but he was nowhere to be seen. The worthy companion quickly grasped that his boss did not want to be found. "Mr. Laughton is not with me," he answered the silent question Cristina was burning to ask.

Trying to hide her embarrassment at her housekeeper's amused expression, Cristina introduced her to Eugênio. And as they seemed to immediately connect in their knowledge and experience of open markets and produce, the girl resumed her casual inspection of the colorful merchandise offered in the many stalls. At the end of a quarter of an hour, Eugênio gallantly made his excuses and departed.

"Such a nice gentleman," Maria murmured with dreamy eyes while she watched him walk away. "And German, too," she said and turned to find Cristina's eyes on her. "From the same region my family comes from, I mean," she quickly added, looking away and starting to walk back home.

"Really?" Cristina chuckled. "And I have never seen his blue eyes so...so soft and warm, you know," she continued, imparting a dreamy tone in her voice.

Maria stole a look at her but said nothing. Yet, as he was from the same city she came from, what could be more natural than that they felt drawn together, she asked herself. She prepared herself for the teasing Cristina would certainly submit her to when she told her she and Eugênio were to meet that evening at the movie theater.

* * *

Maria walked fast down the sidewalk of the Nossa Senhora de Copacabana Avenue. Her destination was not far, the *Cinema Americano*, number 743 in that thoroughfare. It was late afternoon but the sun still shone unabatedly; yet she was so excited that the little beads of perspiration forming on her forehead did not bother her. She tightly held her clutch against her chest with one gloved hand, and with the other patted her freshly bobbed hair that had been expertly tucked under the hat by Cristina.

"Silly child," she mumbled to herself, shaking her head, amused.

She had protested but had finally submitted to the siege held by both mother and daughter who were intent on preparing her for what they deemed a date. It was in vain that she explained that she was just going to the local theater, as she did frequently on Saturday afternoons; that it was merely a rerun of Valentino's *The Sheik*; that Eugênio had simply mentioned that he also planned to be at the theater at a similar time. But a date they called it and a date it was to be. With the help of her teasing mother, Cristina had insisted on also painting Maria's lips. What would her parents have thought if they could have seen her were they alive, Maria wondered. She drew a line on the rouge: she would not permit Cristina to apply it to her cheeks.

Her eyes kept on the pavement, Maria walked utterly aware of the stares of men who passed by her, alone or in pairs. Her heart leaped inside her chest as she approached the theater and discerned a strongly built man, his blond hair shiny with brilliantine, a carnation tucked in the lapel of his pristine white linen suit, a panama in his hand—Eugênio!

"Miss Maria," he greeted her with a slight bowing of the head. After greetings and exchanging a few comments about the weather, he pulled a silver chain and glanced at his watch, tucking it back in an expert gesture. "Shall we go in?" he asked, gallantly offering her his arm.

"Sure," she said nervously. "I must make sure I get back home in time. Miss Cristina has an assignment with the owner of the Copacabana Palace tonight," she said proudly. "One of his private parties."

He smiled and nodded understanding, and both entered the theater.

\* \* \*

A story goes that at the shores of the Titicaca Lake, the Incas built a temple and called it *Copac Ahuana* that in the ancient Peruvian idiom, Quíchua, meant "blue belvedere." The Spanish *conquistadores* transformed the temple into a church and there they installed an image of the Virgin Mary, Our Lady of Copacabana. In the Seventeenth Century, silver merchants brought to Rio a statue of the saint. On the south side of its bay, in a rocky arm of land that pierced the sea—and the Tamoio Indians called Sacopenopã, bird with large feathers—the image found a home: the humble little chapel of Copacabana. In 1908 the chapel was torn down, and by 1914 the Copacabana Fort had been built in its place. On the dawn of June 5th, 1922, the peaceful neighborhood of Copacabana was witness to the Lieutenants' Revolt, when lieutenants Siqueira Campos and Eduardo Gomes, revolting against the "Old Republic", took over the fort.

But the best thing to ever happen to Copacabana was the construction of the Copacabana Palace Hotel. It was not ready for the 1922 International Exhibition that commemorated the 100th anniversary of Brazil's Independence from Portugal, but it opened only in August of 1923. Joseph Gire, a French architect, conceived its façade inspired by two hotels: Negresco in Nice and Carlton in Cannes. The cement used to build the hotel was imported from Germany. Chandeliers and glasses from Czechoslovak, Italian marble, Swedish furniture, British rugs, Baccarat crystals, and Limoges porcelain filled the large rooms with luxury and created tradition. The owner, Octávio Guinle, attracted to his hotel many from the troupe of Escoffier, the famous chef of the London Savoy

Hotel. A law, passed while the Copacabana Palace was still under construction, made the hotel's casino illegal. But its theater, two restaurants, six ballrooms, and 230 rooms kept the more than one thousand employees busy and brought immense wealth. Since its beginning the Copa, as it was affectionately called by the *Cariocas*, established itself as a grand success. By 1924 it had hosted important guests, such as the Lords Bessborrough, Ridley, and Lovat, American entrepreneur Percival Farquhar, and British politician Edwin S. Montagu.

Every time Cristina entered the large hall of the Copa, a wave of pleasure invaded her. It was the same awed feeling on the night of the hotel inauguration. Then securing an invitation through Daniel, she met and even exchanged a few words with the guest of honor, the French dancer Mistinguett, whose legs had been insured in 1919 for half a million Francs. To the disappointment of the many gentlemen present, Mistinguett's legs were carefully tucked away under her long skirt. That night Cristina was introduced and fell in love with one of the Copa's signatures, the special caviar, Guinle's pride: *grand grain, gris, sans sel.*

As on many prior occasions, she was there now to play for Octávio Guinle who had organized a party *en petit comité*. While she walked through the marble corridors she glimpsed angles of her image reflected in the pristine mirrors, and they confirmed that she was impeccably dressed. Other than her performance qualities, her appearance and manners had been her best introduction to the refined hotelier, to whom professionalism and discretion were qualities expected of anyone working for the Copa. He was known amongst employees for his rigid principles of excellence and was often seen during his daily rounds throughout the hotel to stroke the furniture with his fingers looking for dust. It was not uncommon to find him bending over a rug to collect lint. Eighteen rigorous rules made his "Employee Code of Conduct," yet notwithstanding his inflexibility, he was respected and beloved by his subordinates.

A few days after her father died, Cristina had gone to work. Guinle found her a trifle too pale, but the discreet young lady had said nothing. The following day he was told of her loss, so it was not surprising that she found a special place in his practical yet soft heart. He would have given her a permanent job in the hotel but for his mistaken belief that she belonged to a well-to-do family—after all, she lived in a large house on the Atlântica Avenue and had never allowed him or anyone in the hotel to learn of her financial distress.

In the case of Daniel, as he frequented her house, he had guessed it from the things he saw disappear from the rooms—the culprit, he concluded, was the cost of her father's medical treatment. Daniel knew Guinle would have been touched and likely tried to help Cristina, but in his selfishness he could not even think of sharing his ex-pupil's wellbeing. Daniel had actually counted on these very problems to incline Cristina to accept his marriage proposal, and her rebuke had been a hard setback. He found comfort in the mistaken thought that, had he done it through her mother, she might have persuaded Cristina to accept him.

Cristina took the elevator to the sixth floor and knocked on the door of Mr. Guinle's residence, one of the two suites on that floor. A waiter opened the door, and Cristina entered the sumptuously decorated suite where the set table was covered with a starched, immaculately white tablecloth. The Limoges china and the Baccarat crystal reflected the highly polished silverware. From a tiered silver center-piece, suspended tropical flowers formed a multicolored cascade. Octávio Guinle, who with a serious countenance had been inspecting the arrangements at the table, looked at his watch: eight-thirty p.m. sharp. He smiled at her and motioned to the waiter to help her with her stack of papers to the piano.

"*Bonsoir, Mademoiselle*," he nodded, addressing her in French. The young woman had a flawless accent and he enjoyed speaking with her in that language.

"*Bonsoir, Monsieur* Guinle," she returned and continued in French: "Would you like to go through our choice of music for tonight?" and she prayed to God he didn't. Solange, her partner, had not yet arrived and the music sheets they had selected were all with her.

"No, I trust your taste, *Mademoiselle*." (Proud were the ones who could claim Octávio Guinle's absolute trust.) "I know you are going to delight us with your performance. But," he looked around, "I don't see your partner." With a tinge of irritation he turned his eyes to the watch once more. "That young lady seems to

84

never be on time. To her credit, I must admit, she is a master with the violin," he added.

Cristina pleaded: "She has to take two different trams to get here. She lives so far away."

"She should leave home earlier," and added as an afterthought: "or find work closer to where she lives." Then he turned a softer countenance to Cristina: "I knew *you* would be here promptly. Now, since you have time before the guests arrive, I will send some refreshment your way." With a gesture he indicated a chair and a small table that stood between two opened windows: "Please, sit there, Mademoiselle." She thanked him and he left her to beckon a waiter.

A few minutes later a small dish of caviar surrounded by crispy melba toast and a bubbling flute of champagne were placed on the table beside her. Guinle's interpretation of *some refreshment* was very much reflective of his lifestyle.

This was one of the few occasions when Cristina enjoyed consuming alcohol; the dry champagne complemented the taste of the caviar. She searched for Guinle with her eyes to thank him for his generosity, but he was already gone, certainly to give his toilette the final touches. Not fifteen minutes had elapsed since Cristina had arrived when the entrance door was opened and a stocky girl with abundant black curls forced under a cloche hat entered, her chubby hands encumbered with music books. Solange rushed in and a broad smile exposed wide teeth that overwhelmed a small mouth of narrow lips.

As she made a beeline to Cristina, a door opened and in came Solange's nemesis, Octávio Guinle. He spotted her and his look of disapproval, though mild, was unmistakable. Her already large eyes widened farther as Solange saw him. "Mr. Guinle," she hesitated and, encumbered with her violin box, anxious to approach him to excuse herself for her tardiness, tripped and the papers she carried slipped to the floor, littering the rug. She stood there frozen by her clumsiness.

With a soft gasp Cristina jumped to her feet, and, joining the girl, quickly helped her gather the sparse papers in one pile. "It is all right," she whispered trying to reassure her friend. "He is not going to eat you, Solange."

"Isn't he," was the whispered retort.

"Come with me." Cristina motioned with her head to a corner where a piano and a music stand stood. "Sit down and take a sip of this," she said and handed her the second serving of champagne she had just been offered by the waiter.

Solange sipped the drink and her eyes widened. "Oh, this is good." She licked her lips and took a longer sip. "What's this? Champagne?" Cristina, fearing she was having too much too quickly, took the glass back. "Oh, but 'tis good stuff, ain't it?"

"Yes, 'tis good stuff, but 'tis not water, my girl." Cristina shook her finger at her friend, teasingly. "If you drink it too quickly, you will end up drunk, and that is the last thing we need to happen. Now, shall we sort through the music and put them in the order we will play?"

After a few minutes, they had the sequence of the pieces ready.

"They were all separated, Cristina, I swear. Well, until I dropped them on the floor, like an idiot," Solange lamented. "I always do everything wrong when *he* is near," she said and indicated Guinle with a quick motion of her eyebrows, not daring to raise her eyes.

Cristina patted the girl's shoulder, trying to comfort her. Poor Solange suffered from a malady that affected many a member of the Copa staff, and she jokingly called 'guinlephobia'; but beside the awe of her employer and the shyness the girl felt when he was around, Cristina suspected another feeling was the real cause of Solange's problem. She was amused to imagine Mr. Guinle's shock were he ever to guess what was actually behind the girl's clumsiness. At that thought she stifled a chuckle. Solange raised an inquisitive eye to her, but Cristina merely nodded her head and, turning to the piano, took her place while Solange stroked a few cords of her violin.

"Why don't you play something, just to warm up?" Cristina encouraged her knowing that once the girl started playing, all troubles would be forgotten. And as Solange played, the violin's heavenly melody seemed to be brought in by the night's breeze that filtered through the opened windows.

A few minutes later people started trickling in, and, while playing, both Cristina and Solange took the time to observe them. Among them a man who came marching in attracted the girls' attention. His bushy eyebrows topped fierce dark eyes that seemed even darker due to the pallor of his skin. A big mustache almost completely hid his mouth, the whole making him look like a walrus. His embonpoint was somewhat masked by an overinflated chest and rigid spine. Amused, the girls' eyes met and the similarity of their expressions was disconcerting. They ignored that he was Bogdan Zietarski, manager of a stud farm for His Royal Highness Prince Roman Wladyslaw Sanguszko of Poland. He was returning from a visit to the stud farms in South of Brazil—an area reputed for the special qualities of the grass.

Suddenly Cristina recognized Robert among them. Beside him stood a tall woman, a diamond tiara holding back her wavy, bobbed red hair. Her tanned bosom regaled all eyes through the low neckline of her dress. The back of the dress plunged perilously close to the base of her spine, revealing the satiny curve of her waist. Her white teeth gleamed while Guinle bent over her hand where diamonds sparkled. She was a wealthy American heiress visiting Rio. During one of his visits to the hotel, Robert was introduced by Guinle to this glamorous compatriot, rich Sarah Wilkins-Barth, a New York socialite, who he knew from pictures in the papers. Her father, Thornton Wilkins-Barth was the owner of a super-market empire—the Wilkins-Barth & Sons, Inc. Without knowing exactly how it had happened, Robert found himself bound to accompany Sarah to dinner that Saturday.

Cristina's heart missed a beat as Robert's hand held the red-haired siren's elbow. When his eyes suddenly met hers, she turned away, but not quickly enough to miss his smile. That was what she gained for watching the guests when she should have been working!

Turning a sulky countenance to Solange, she pointed at the page in front of her: "Chopin's Prelude No. 4." Not knowing what to make of Cristina's expression, the girl nodded. A last look was exchanged and they started in unison, the melody's moving tones a perfect background to the room's setup. Prelude No. 4 was followed by No. 7.

But the more Cristina tried to ignore Robert's presence, the more aware of him she became. With his back to her, he could not see the many times her eyes focused on him and his dining companion. Cristina wished she could have an entire orchestra play

Beethoven's 5$^{th}$—squeezed into the almost nonexistent gap between Robert and his partner's shoulders. Would she handle the drums with gusto! When during coffee one of Sibelius's Pensees Lyriques brought their first round to a close, Robert excused himself and, turning to face the performers, broke into applause. The others followed his lead. Solange blushed, never comfortable at being the center of attention, and Cristina graciously bowed her head.

Hiding her irritation, Cristina took advantage of the pause to approach the window farthest in the room from the guests. She hoped the fresh air would help calm the unreasonable feelings that had been assailing her since Robert had arrived with the red-haired woman. But why should she even mind what Robert did? That flaming-headed stick could sit on his lap for all she cared! But inside her, a tiny voice–which she adamantly dismissed—told her that whatever he did, she would find highly relevant. "Nonsense," she mumbled.

"Nonsense?"

Robert's voice took her so much by surprise that she gave a low gasp. Horrified, she realized she had spoken aloud.

"Nothing," she retorted and felt her face reddening, which exacerbated her discomfort even further. She squared her shoulders and, with her chin held high, decided to face him and meet his amused expression: "Why, you abandoned your partner, Mr. Laughton. It seems she lost her balance without your…your propping presence," she said with visible irritation, only to regret it.

What a lovely discovery: the little doe was jealous. "I beg your pardon, Miss Cristina," he told her with such an amused tone that the redness in her cheeks deepened. "I thought you only had eyes for your piano. Had I any idea the young lady's proximity to me bothered you, I would have avoided her," and the glee in his eyes could not escape her.

She was so outraged she could barely answer in a steady voice: "You estimate your seductive powers too highly, Mr. Laughton. I am willing to bet the lady will certainly have forgotten you by tomorrow," she retorted in a futile attempt to upset him.

"Oh, a bet," he teased her, and, bending nearer, lowered his tone: "I simply cannot resist. Now, what should we bet?"

His eyes twinkled with mischief, and her response was to turn on her heels and leave him alone by the window. She was jealous, he thought. And, surprisingly, the idea pleased him because that meant she did care for him.

"Here you are, darling," Sarah's voice interrupted the train of his thoughts. "Will you come to my room? We are forming a game party," she said as her teasing eyes rose to his. "Will you come?"

As Robert left the room with Sarah, an adaptation for piano and violin of Giovanni Bottesini Elegy No. 2, "Romanza Patetica," pierced the air. And throughout the rest of the evening, Cristina kept her moist eyes on the piano keys.

* * *

The sea breeze lightly played with Robert's tousled hair. The early morning sky slowly overtook darkness and helped delineate the foaming waves. Robert took a deep breath. The window of the Copacabana Palace hotel room formed a frame to the beautiful beach spreading far to the brightening horizon.

Why did I stay here, he asked himself. The prior night, after a nice poker game, Sarah begged him to stay. Having had too much Champaign than was good for her, she poured her latest romantic escapade into Robert's unwilling and bored ears. After years collecting (and discarding) love affairs, and if he understood her slurred confidences, the girl had fallen head over heels in love with some Sicilian guy. The sentiment, he was told, was vastly reciprocated. But her suitor, as was common among the natives of that part of Italy, was as jealous as Othello and kept her in tenterhooks, fearing some volcanic eruption every time her eyes casually fell on another man. They had recently parted after a terrible fight when he promised she would never see him again. Robert handed her his handkerchief, which she returned stained with makeup, and tried to impart some words of wisdom, which he did not really have, and ended up spending the rest of the night with his fingers entwined in hers while she slept peacefully and he fell into a restless sleep.

A few minutes in front of the bathroom mirror had restored some respectability to his hair when a knock was heard on the door. What to do? He did not want to be caught in Sarah's room and damage her reputation—supposing she had any to be damaged. The knocks became more insistent.

"*Sarah, amore mio, sono io,* Andrea," a melodious male voice insinuated itself through the crevices of the door.

She sat up in the bed, suddenly wide awake, her white dress crumpled, reflecting the outside light. Her somnolent, disturbed eyes turned to Robert. "No," she whispered with a desperate gesture to quiet him. "It's my fiancé Andrea," she whispered in confusion.

"This is getting better and better," he said and his eyebrow lifted.

"Sarah, Sarah, wake up and open the door, *bella*," the voice continued with a heavy Italian accent.

"What to do." The girl anxiously petted her hair and, getting off the bed, tried to restore some order to her dress.

"Well, I would be delighted if I could stay longer and meet your beau, but unfortunately I must go," he answered, not trying to hide his amusement.

"I know, I know!" She turned to him, a harassed look in her eyes. "You must go and go *now*." Pulling him by the arm, she rushed to one of the large windows "From here you can get to the next room and..."

"What? Are you out of your mind? Don't count on that," he cut her off. "Besides, we did nothing wrong, so I will leave through the door and you and your fiancé can sort things out when I'm gone."

"Oh, you don't know Andrea," she said and tightened the grip on his arm. "He will kill you if he thinks you spent the night here. Quick, under the bed," and she started pulling him by the arm.

"I am not going to hide under your bed. I have a better idea," he grinned and before she could stop him, began walking to the door

"You're not going to open that door," she said with a voice that fear had turned into a choked whisper.

"Watch me," he said and opened it wide.

A pair of startled black eyes stared at Robert, found Sarah in the background, and then angrily darted back at Robert, measuring him from head to foot. "And who may you be, Sir," Andrea asked, his eyes narrowed, his eyebrows knitted together.

"Just a friend, Andrea. It's not what you think." And grasping one of the man's hands, Robert brought him into Sarah's room while maneuvering himself out of it. "I wish I had time for a chat, but I am sure you and Sarah have a lot to catch up on, and, you know, three is a crowd. It was nice meeting you. So long, *ciao*," he waived at the two people who watched him with stunned expressions and left, closing the door behind him.

As he strolled down the corridor, he could hear the man's loud baritone voice. That was a close one, he thought, but he had come out of it unscathed.

\* \* \*

After leaving Ramires and Dulce, the thought of how to use the knowledge he had acquired would not leave Daniel's mind. The next day, knowing of Cristina's assignment at the Copacabana Palace Hotel, he decided to try his luck again in a "chance" meeting with her. So in the evening he took a tram to Copacabana and alighted at Nossa Senhora de Copacabana Avenue and walked to Cristina's house. As he checked his watch, he realized he would have a long while to wait until Guinle's dinner party was over—he knew they could last until the small hours of the morning. He looked for a suitable place in the shadows to wait.

The house was quiet and shrouded in darkness. He did not know how long he had stood there, his eyes on the house, not really seeing it. He then retraced his steps to in front of the Copacabana Palace, where, crossing the street to the beach, he sat on the sand to ruminate on the information he had stored. Still deep in thought, the first morning lights surprised him. He decided to go into the hotel to see if he could get some breakfast. He sneaked in and, walking through its long corridors, suddenly saw the unmistakable silhouette of Robert come down the stairs.

He stood for several minutes, recovering from the surprise of seeing Robert cross the lobby and leave the hotel, and was wondering about the American's presence there, when he saw another man charge down the marble stairs and, looking around wildly, land at the unsuspecting concierge like a tornado.

"*Dov'è quel maledeto*?" Andrea's voice thundered throughout the hotel lobby as he pounded the counter with a tight fist. A couple of early risers, who had just gone downstairs to go for a swim at the beach, turned their heads in surprise.

"I beg your pardon, sir," the impeccably dressed concierge asked, concealing his disapproval at the gentleman's behavior under his impassive demeanor. He knew Mr. Guinle would be livid if he heard that one of his employees could not handle a disgruntled guest.

Andrea took a deep breath and, collecting himself, repeated the question in heavily accented Portuguese: "Where is that scoundrel?"

"What scoundrel, sir?" the concierge asked, calmly.

"The tall man who just passed by," Andrea almost screamed, provoked by the man's placidity. "You couldn't have possibly missed him," he added, thinking of Robert's tall stature.

By then the other employee at the reception counter had quietly faded into the background, leaving the concierge to deal with the situation alone.

It was clear that the concierge had no intention of answering the questions put to him. Daniel decided to take advantage of the situation and interfered: "Excuse me, sir," at which the Italian turned a charged countenance to him. "I apologize for butting in, but are you referring to the tall, blond man who left a few minutes before you came downstairs?"

Andrea's thunderous countenance relaxed a bit. "Have you seen him?" he asked Daniel without preamble. "Did you see in which direction he went?"

"My name is Daniel Cabral," was the answer. Daniel extended a hand to Andrea that went ignored. "Why don't we sit down and we can talk about it?"

"*Senti*, I don't have time for chitchat. If you know who the American is and where he went, just tell me and I will be on my way!"

"I believe you are referring to Mr. Laughton," he answered slowly, realizing that the more he made him wait, the more Andrea fumed—and the worse it would be for Robert. "He is staying on a yacht called *Anne Louise*." He paused, increasing the other's irritation.

"And where can I find this blasted yacht?" Andrea questioned with a nasty look in his eye, the little bit of patience he had almost all gone.

"It is anchored somewhere near the harbor, downtown. I am sure it won't be difficult to find." And Daniel grinned as the man turned on his heels and ran out of the hotel. Whoever that was, it was certainly someone with a grudge against Robert. He did not care what grievance it was, only that he had sent trouble on the American's way.

# CHAPTER 6

After tossing and turning for many hours, Cristina decided to get out of bed. Pacing around her bedroom seemed not to be the tonic she needed, so wide awake, she dressed in a light frock and went down to the garden, where the night breeze felt good. Walking to the front of the house, she opened the gate and looked around: nobody was in sight, the sidewalks were completely deserted. She stepped out and, slowly and unconsciously, started walking in the direction of the Copacabana Palace. From there she could hear the murmur of the waves' cadenced splash over the soft sand; it was comforting and muffled the sound of her footsteps. The first morning light fought with the light-poles and won the battle, annihilating the perfect circles that, just a few moments before, were printed on the pavement stones. Oblivious of her surroundings, Cristina did not notice that, in the sky, the darkness was slowly washed away by waves of liquid gold and pink that timidly morphed into light blue, which did not yet reflect the color of the indigo sea. She just kept putting a foot ahead of the other, deep in thought.

When the night before Robert had left the party with the red-haired woman, she felt as if the air had gone out of the room; she feared she would suffocate. Her heart thundered so it sounded to her louder than the music played by Solange and her, whose notes seemed to dissolve undetected to her. She had to force herself to keep playing. Then she felt furious, outraged even—but at herself, at the inexplicable ascendancy this man she barely knew

94

had over her. She felt helpless and uncertain of her own reactions. What kind of power was it that he possessed, which made her feel awkward and silly? When he was near she was sure she would not protest if he took her in his arms—as that evening in his boat had proven. But, there, he had left with another woman and had not even looked back at her…

And now, her heart was again being deluged by the same chaotic feelings; they were back in all their strength, tearing at her chest, their merciless claws scratching at her tired, bruised eyes. She kept walking slowly, feeling alternately miserable and outraged, hating and adoring Robert, vowing to extract him from her heart at any cost and, in the same breath, to follow him to the ends of the earth. Oh, those eyes, that crooked smile—if he only knew their power… And then she suddenly lifted her head and saw the very man materialize several feet ahead of her. She froze in place, as if cemented to the ground. He did not see her but adjusted his hat and, turning to the left, walked away.

For a moment she thought of following him, but he was walking too fast. Besides, if he saw her, how would she explain her presence there, alone, at that time? But what was *he* doing there, at that time, coming out of the hotel? Time stood still as her mind revolved only around those thoughts. And suddenly the realization hit her that he was coming out of the hotel because he had spent the night with the red-haired woman. The thought hit her with an almost physical pain, making her lose balance. Her tight fist held her lips from trembling, but as she could not deter them, tears rolled down her cheeks, blurring the view of him. Wretchedly, she faltered and held on to a fence, trying to find something to steady herself. She felt cheated. Yet down inside a thought crept through the maze of her thoughts, that she could not accuse Robert of doing anything wrong. He was a bachelor and had the right to be with whomever he chose. Besides, he had never given her false hopes.

In this state of mind, she directed her steps back home and quietly went to her bedroom where, the door closed, she crumpled onto bed and succumbed to a paroxysm of tears. She hid her face in the pillow to stifle the sound of her sobs. And this was how Maria found her not long afterwards. Unlike Brazilian servants, she did not sleep in a remote part of the house but in a bedroom between Cristina's and her mother's. She had heard the young woman leave and got out of bed, and, wrapped in a housecoat, awaited the girl's return, wondering what had happened.

"What is it, Cristina, my child?" Maria whispered, bending beside the bed. As she got no answer, she sat down and then coaxed Cristina into her arms. The young woman let herself melt into that comforting embrace, resting her head on Maria's shoulder, while abundant tears fell from her eyes. "Shh, shh, it will be all right. What is it, my pet, tell me," she asked again, even more gently.

Still tightly holding Maria, in a muffled voice cut by sobs and sniffs, Cristina told of her early morning escapade. Maria shook her head and, holding the girl's chin, gently forced her to look up and started drying her tear-streaked face.

"Ain't you a silly little girl?" she asked while her heart went out to her darling girl. "Let me tell you a bit about the world: that is how men are, my pet. Without blinking they go with the first good-looking skirt that offers herself to them. But that," she quickly added, cutting off Cristina before she could protest, "that doesn't mean they are in love with the skirt in case, you know." She laughed quietly. "The thing is, child, that they think less with this head," she tapped her forehead, "than with the other one—you know what I mean." She winked one eye at a scandalized Cristina. Never had she heard Maria speak so openly about such matters. "Now if he was committed to you and had gone after the skinny siren, *I* would go myself and have a talk with Mr. American! I don't care if he can't speak Portuguese because he'd understand me plenty," she said, menacingly holding a tight fist in the air.

Cristina could not help but be amused at the thought of Maria cuffing Robert. Only Maria's blunt talk could make her laugh at such an occasion. "How do you know she was skinny, Maria?" she asked, sniffing and drying her tears with a handkerchief Maria had produced from the depths of her housecoat's pocket.

"Oh, but aren't all these flappers a bundle of bones held together by some skin?" Maria asked, with a surprised expression and a dismissive gesture of the hands. "And since this American fell for you, child, it can only mean that he prefers them skinny. Now you quit these silly thoughts," she commanded, rising from the bed after giving Cristina a peck on the brow. "Enough of this drama, unless you want a part in Mr. Valentino's next movie! You go wash your face like the good girl you are. I'm gonna run to the Estábulo Mimoso to buy some fresh milk, as we're out. Then we can go to church together after a good breakfast. It will do you good to ask guidance from higher, right? By the time you fix your bed and wash yourself, I'll be back and coffee will be ready." She turned at the door and added: "And remember, child, that people make mistakes all the time. Even you," she winked a mischievous eye at Cristina and softly closed the door behind her.

Maria was probably right. It would be good to sit in a quiet place and pray. And she was right, too, that people were imperfect and that did not make them bad—but it sure did not make it easier to accept these imperfections...

* * *

Desiree sat up, stunned, as Robert told her where he had been that night.

"You must be mad, Robbie!" her voice quivered in anger. "How could you spend the night with a woman you barely knew and tell me all about it so calmly? And laugh about it to boot," she snapped at him.

"I didn't know you'd become a moralist." Robert stretched his long legs before him, sat back on the chair and, with a content sigh, calmly sipped his coffee. "Are you planning a long sermon? Because I have things I must do, you know, so make it brief."

"Oh, don't be silly!" She threw her napkin at the table and stood up almost overturning her chair. "Who knows, Sarah might be after a rich husband!" Her eyes widened at the thought and she turned to him a horrified countenance.

"And I thought you wanted to see me married," he murmured, shaking his head, a twinkle of amusement in his eyes. "As far as I know, if there is something Sarah does not need, honey, it's money. Did I just rhyme? I am positively waxing poetic this morning," he said with a beatific expression, then with a suspicious look at her: "What are you doing awake this early? It seems it's becoming a habit with you," he mumbled.

She looked away, embarrassed. "You didn't come back to the boat last night—remember? Well, I was sure there was some charity girl[ii] involved…”

"Now, Desiree, is that a way a lady should be talking? Tsk, tsk, tsk," he faked a disapproving air.

She stuck her tongue out at him then continued: "Then Bunky told me… Oh, well, fine: I *asked* him, I admit," she snapped, seeing Robert's amused expression," and he told me you were going to meet that walking corpse by the name of Sarah. Oh, don't you make light of it, Robert," she snapped at his chuckling. "This Sarah is not from my circle of friends, but I know enough about her love affairs and shenanigans," she nodded with a serious countenance to give force to her statement.

"Oh, would you stop this nonsense? Nothing happened," he pleaded. "Bunky already fills the part of a chaperon; I don't need another."

"Oh, Robert, you're such a boob sometimes, I despair of you," she almost screamed, stamping her foot in fury when Robert, who could no longer contain himself, burst out laughing. "Haven't you heard of Sarah's behavior? Her scandals are quite frequent in the gossip columns—and she enjoys her notoriety, which means she would not mind dragging you through the mud!"

At that Robert almost choked on the coffee he was drinking. "And you are afraid she could soil my maidenly reputation? I see." And he added, pensively: "Desiree, you definitely should start writing. In fact," he sat up, "that sounds like a great idea. Have you ever considered writing as a profession? One thing you have in abundance is time…"

"Why are you trying to dismiss my concerns," she asked in exasperation. "Oh, you monster," she snapped. "You are just doing this to tease me," and she struck his chest with a closed fist as he continued to laugh.

"So long as it keeps you off my back—and off the backs of the other poor, unsuspecting souls you plan to torment," he answered, barely avoiding her fist again. "I am telling you, nothing happened, goose. Believe me. How many times have I lied to you?"

She pursed her lips, closed her eyes, and began counting on the fingers of one hand. When she started on the other hand, he gently shook her by the shoulders.

"Listen here, girlie. She merely wanted someone to confide

in. She was upset because her latest beau did what no other ever dared: he broke up with her."

"Now, that is what I call news: Sarah, dumped!" She relished the thought. "And you, playing father confessor—yeah, sure! Anyway, I told you what I think, so don't you come to me later asking my advice."

"And when have I ever asked your advice, you brat?" he asked her with raised eyebrows.

She clicked her tongue, and turning away from him, sat down and picked up a book—*Mah Jong and How to Play it* by Etienne—just to drop it almost immediately, standing up to resume pacing around the room in deep thought.

Robert eyed the book discretely. At least it was the new fad, the Mah Jong game; she had finally dropped her fascination with the Ouija boards. He grabbed the paper and started sipping his coffee.

Entrenched behind his paper, Robert concluded that, after what had just happened, what Desiree needed was a child. That would definitely solve his problem and would give her a real baby to pamper. He would have to have a serious talk with Max. And soon!

His train of thought was interrupted by a commotion coming from the deck. He dropped the paper and went topside. He was followed by Desiree and Bunky, who had entered the room with more fresh coffee. On deck they found two crewmen holding a disheveled man. Puffing and screaming, he kept the crew busy.

"What is going on?" Robert asked. As he approached the group, he recognized the disheveled man being held: Andrea, Sarah's fiancé.

Before the crew knew what was happening, and without a word, Andrea freed himself and charged at Robert like an angry bull. Desiree, not far from where Robert stood, let out a strangled shriek. Distracted by his cousin and caught by surprise, Robert was barely able to avert the man's right hook, and his ring lightly grazed Robert's left chin. With a quick spin, and using the momentum of Andrea's body, he managed to place himself behind his attacker, who had momentarily lost balance, and tightly pinning the man's arms behind his back, commanded: "Calm down! What's with you, pal? Are you mad?! It's all right, I've got him," he told the crewmen who were trying to assist. As Andrea realized he was outnumbered, Robert felt his muscles relax under his grip. "I am going to let you go, but no sudden moves, or you will go for an early swim!"

Freed, an infuriated Andrea faced Robert. His tie and coat were askew and his pomaded hair had been badly compromised during the struggle. As he adjusted the lapels back into place and tried to fix the tie, the remains of the carnation in the buttonhole was furiously thrown overboard.

"Now that you have calmed down, would you mind explaining this operatic invasion of private property?" Robert asked, distractedly pushing away Desiree, who had approached him and was trying to inspect his grazed chin. He pushed her hand away, exasperated.

"You soiled the honor of my fiancé. I stand here to challenge you to a duel, Mr. Laughton," Andrea answered with an arrogant tilt of the head.

"A duel," Desiree echoed, baffled.

"Yes, a duel," he turned his contorted face to her. "This man," and he made a dramatic gesture towards Robert, "has dishonored me and I demand satisfaction!"

All heads turned to Robert, who suddenly felt an incredible urge to laugh but controlled himself.

"C'mon, Andrea! You can't be serious. This is the Twentieth, not the Eighteen Century," he dismissed it with a bored expression. "And nothing happened. Sarah just wanted to talk— and talk about you, you oaf!"

"No," Andrea took a step closer to him, a fist in the air: "you will not escape my *vendetta*! The house of Calvetti has been soiled and I, one of its honored representatives, demand satisfaction!" He was visibly working himself again to a state of exasperation.

"Well, if your house has been, as you say, *soiled*," and a smile twisted Robert's mouth, "it seems to me you need a cleaning crew."

"Now you insult me!"

"Not in the least," was the smooth answer. Then serious: "You invade my property, make the biggest ruckus, take a swing at me without even giving me a chance to speak, and accuse *me* of insulting you!"

"Please, Robbie, don't upset the gentleman further."

He heard Desiree's frantic whispers beside him and ignored her. Bunky, who had been slowly approaching the scene, stopped at a barely noticeable gesture from Robert.

"I demand—do you hear me?—I *demand* satisfaction and will not leave until you agree to a place, time, and weapons," Andrea barked, ignoring Desiree's pleas and thrusting two menacing fists at the morning breeze.

Suddenly, inside Robert's mischievous brain, a thought started to take shape. "You won't leave, huh?" he asked, rubbing his injured chin while mentally developing a plan. He had to stifle a chuckle as he turned a deadpan face to Andrea: "Fine, let us finish this here and now!"

"Robbie," Desiree lunged at him, grabbing his arm and shaking it violently. "Are you out of your mind?"

"Trust me," he assured her in a low voice.

"Good," Andrea answered, a bit surprised at Robert's abrupt change of mind. "Do you have gentlemen's weapons on board?"

"But of course," Robert assure him. "And since you were the one who threw down the gauntlet, I have the right to choose the weapons. I don't know how you duel in Italy, but that's how the rule goes in the US, and you happen to be on an American vessel," he gestured at the American flag.

"Very well, choose your weapons then, Mr. Laughton!"

"I have a feeling you might regret this," Desiree told Andrea, seeing the furtive smile in her cousin's face.

Andrea did not have time to give her words any thought, for Robert was already putting things in motion. "Since you won't have the chance of picking a second of your choice, may I suggest Mr. Griffith," he motioned to his valet, Bunky, who, at these words, silently joined Robert.

Andrea eyed the man suspiciously, but in such an awkward situation, he relented and gave a slight nod. Besides, it made no difference since this was just a mere formality—and so long as he was able to settle the situation with that *figlio di puttana*, he would have had the Devil as a second if he offered!

"My second," Robert said and turned to Desiree.

"A woman!" Andrea gasped, scandalized. "But it is impossible!"

"Listen, pal, you came to my boat cuffing everyone in your way, screaming bloody murder with demands of satisfaction; are you going to chicken out now?" he asked a red-faced Andrea, who, with inflated chest and stretched spine, had no remedy but to agree to a female second with what shred of pride was left him.

"Very well," the Italian finally answered, haughtily.

"Then let's get this over with, shall we? Now, the weapons…"

He beckoned to Eugênio to approach; he had been drawn from his kitchen by the noise and stood by watching in silence. Tony, mimicking his attitude, placidly sat on his haunches, following everything with a cool eye. Robert confabulated with the man for a few seconds and, letting him go, turned to his audience.

"The, er, weapons will be brought up here momentarily. There will be a single volley for each of us." As Andrea approved, pleased, Robert concluded the Italian was obviously a good shot. "After each of us has taken his shot, no matter the outcome, satisfaction will have been given. Are you agreeable to these terms?"

"Yes," Andrea answered while Bunky helped him out of his jacket.

"Are you mad, Robert," Desiree whispered at him when they had distanced themselves. "Pistols? And since when are pistols kept in this canoe?"

He smiled while removing the cuff-links from his shirt. Depositing them in Desiree's shaky hands, he rolled up his sleeves. "Well, I do have weapons on board. Do you think I'd navigate the seven seas without protection?" He smiled at her horrified expression. "Now, you might want to keep some distance, so not to get splattered."

"What? Splattered… Oh, my God, by blood, you mean?" She wailed as the import of his words bore down on her. "Where is Max when I need him—how can one sleep so heavily?" she moaned and looked around frantically, wringing her hands. It was too late to go down and try to drag her spouse to the melee. "You've lost your mind, Robert! Please, stop this madness at once," she pleaded, almost sobbing, blindly stuffing his cuff-links into one of her pockets.

"Trust me," he said and held her firmly by the arm, looking deeply into her eyes. And what she saw was a mischievous expression she knew so well. "Nobody will get hurt. Will you trust me?" he asked, lightly shaking her by the shoulders. For an answer he got a deep sigh and a headshake.

In the meantime Eugênio had returned to the deck and, followed by a dutiful and quite solemn Tony, placed two small baskets on the floor, near each contender. He imperceptibly bowed his head to Robert and backed away.

Robert approached the basket nearer to him and took an overripe tomato from inside. Andrea, who had approached the other basked, stopped in his tracks, puzzled.

"There, you have the weapons of my choice, Mr. Calvetti: ripe tomatoes at 20 paces!"

Andrea roared with indignation, while Desiree echoed him, but for a different reason: she almost dropped to the floor laughing. Only Robert could have conceived such ridiculously comic plan. "Bravo!" She clapped but could not help feeling a little pity for Andrea, another poor victim of her cousin's less than subtle sense of humor.

"Calm down, Andrea! You agreed in front of witnesses to my terms, now let's get to it, shall we?"

Crushed by the truth of the statement, overwhelmed by the ridiculousness of the trap in which he had fallen—by his own doing, he had to concede—Andrea resigned himself. With the little dignity he could muster, he picked a large, mushy tomato from the basket that a solemn Bunky extended to him. He and Robert walked to the center of the deck to face each other, turned, walked off twenty paces, then faced one another. To Andrea's further exasperation, Robert sported a wide smile and Desiree was almost choking with laughter. Only Bunky Griffith kept a dignified, somewhat aloof, expression.

"You have the first, er, throw, since you are the challenged party," a meek Andrea muttered.

Robert gave him an impious smile, and, taking great pains at mimicking Babe Ruth's wind-up, aimed the biggest tomato Desiree had procured for him, and let it go with all his strength. Andrea, who had stoically closed his eyes, opened them with visible distress. The front of his shirt was splattered with a mass of tomato flesh and seeds that slid down to his pants and dripped on his highly polished shoes.

"Right in the numbers, Robbie," Desiree yelled in a passion, clapping her hands and jumping with excitement.

"Well, I guess it's your turn now. Take your best shot," Robert taunted, and feet apart, firmly planted on the wooden planks of the boat, arms akimbo, he waited.

Recovering from his momentary stupor, and incensed by Robert's goad, Andrea did not think and in a flurry of frustration, threw the tomato pell-mell at his adversary. As the object's trajectory was certainly going to pass clear of him, and to everybody's disbelief, Robert lunged into its path, intercepting the tomato with his chest, where it splattered with a thud. There was a general "ohhh" of disappointment and then utter silence. Suddenly, Andrea's thunderous laugh echoed. Robert started laughing too and both men stepped ahead to meet, and, to Desiree astonishment, exchange a vigorous handshake.

"Men are the goofiest animals I have ever encountered," Desiree exclaimed. "You come close to shooting, challenge each other, threaten to skin each other alive, then, suddenly, start patting yourselves on the back, all smiles… Who can understand you?"

"Unlike women," Robert turned to her, "we know how to forgive and forget," and he winked an eye. Then turning to Andrea: "Now that we settled our differences, may I offer you a clean shirt and, if you didn't yet have it, some breakfast, Andrea?"

"Oh, *si, si*, with pleasure!"

And as they started walking towards the stairs, a somnolent Max came up. "I heard some commotion—." He stopped short, seeing people starting to descend the steps. "What, did I miss something?" he asked, eyeing the red stained shirts and the two smiling men.

"Oh, nothing of much import, darling. These two just decided to make some tomato sauce for tonight; we're going to eat Italian," Desiree informed her perplexed husband.

He watched the two men go down below, followed by Bunky. "And the tomatoes were a bit too ripe, I say!" He turned questioning eyes to his wife. "Do be serious, old girl."

"Oh, just give me a few minutes to recover from these two

and I'll tell you the whole story!"

\* \* \*

Robert's right-hand man, Bunky, was from a once well-to-do family, the Griffiths, from a small town in Ohio—some have it as Huron—that had fallen into hard times. The story goes that Bunky got frisky with the daughter of one of the pillars of local society. Rather than face the music—in this case the Wedding March—he escaped town at night. By crooked ways—which he seemed too frequently to adopt—he landed in New York. After getting into all sorts of trouble with the local constabulary, his life changed when his path crossed Robert's. On an early November day in 1899, Bunky was out in Manhattan in pursuit of some profitable, but mostly irregular, occupation. As he stood to watch an automobile parade go by, he spotted a little boy who, wrenching his hand from a distracted parent, was darting for the busy street. Bunky reached out and caught the child, saving him from being injured. "Where ya going, lil' stinker?" he asked the squirming mite he held with a firm hand. Realizing the treasure he had found in that man capable of controlling his three year-old son—a troublesome little pest *ab ovo*—John Laughton hired him on the spot. Thus Bunky entered Master Robert's life, giving his father much needed respite. Physically, Bunky Griffith was 6'5" of pure muscle, had stone-hard blue eyes, and wore a less flamboyant version of the walrus mustache. Already balding he shaved his head daily, but shamelessly blamed Robert's.

\* \* \*

"Hello, Cris!"

Desiree had entered the music store and made a beeline to Cristina and the girl wondered how she knew where to find her. Had she asked, she would certainly get the truth: that she had haunted Robert for information and was finally able to get it.

"Robbie was coming downtown for some errands, and I decided to join him. I thought I would do some window gazing—I am dying of curiosity to learn all about Brazilian fashion. But before duty, pleasure: I decided to stop by and to convince you to have lunch with me—and, I will not take no for an answer," she added before Cristina could open her mouth. And, grabbing the girl's hand and linking it in her arm, strode out of the store, under the manager's stunned gaze.

"Do not be late, Miss Cristina," she heard the manager say as they approached the store's entrance.

He fished his watch from the waistcoat pocket and took a long look at it. That was a popular girl, he thought, and shook his head. First that American who came to buy music, now this elegant lady, a foreigner, too, from her looks... Well, at least she seemed to attract persons of quality to the store, he pondered and shrugged his shoulders.

"Now, where can we go have a nice, quiet little lunch?" Desiree asked when they found themselves at the sidewalk.

"Oh, my," Cristina laughed. "A quiet lunch downtown at this time of the year? Impossible!"

'Ok, then what about a nice lunch at some extra busy place? The question is: where? I am a helpless foreigner, so I am in your hands, my girl!"

"Perhaps we could go to the Sympathia," Cristina answered after quick consideration. Colombo was out of the question; since her meeting there with Robert, it had become something akin to a shrine, one she would visit alone to secretly daydream of him. "It is close by, and I have one hour, which I am sure will be time enough. Now I cannot get back late. I can't afford to lose this job, Desiree," she added a bit concerned.

"Oh, never mind that; soon you won't need this or any job."

"What do you mean," Cristina asked, bemused.

"Nothing, nothing, just me talking through the back of my head," and with an innocent expression, she looked at an even more confused Cristina, and patted her hand. "Let's go to this Seempacheeah. How do we get there?"

Cristina could not help smiling at her pronunciation. "We go down to that second street over there," she pointed, "the Uruguaiana—then veer left. Sympathia is at the corner of Rosário Street and Central Avenue, just a couple of minutes from here. Shall we go?"

On their way, Desiree was deeply interested in everything

she saw, so different from New York, but did not stop at every store because Cristina's firm grip kept her moving.

At that time of day, Café e Bar Sympathia, as did also Cavé and Colombo, regurgitated customers. That it was located at the corner of Rosário and Central is almost a matter of opinion. The thin neoclassical building facing the wide Central Avenue, was plastered like a buttress against the Nossa Senhora da Conceição e Boa Morte Church, which portal and front were still the same 1784 project by Mestre Valentin. The result was the most unusual combination, as if a slice of the side of a building had been affixed to a somewhat large church.

The outstretched awning that covered the length of the front displayed the establishment's name: *A Sympathia*. Under it a few wicker chairs and tables were scattered at the sidewalk, where customers ate. Desiree spotted a table where an old couple was just leaving. She lunged at it, crossing right in front of two young women who were obviously bent on getting there before her. She sat down and, removing her hat and gloves, turned to the women, who watched with unhappy countenances, and gave them a victorious smile.

"Safe at home," she stated and smiled at their confused looks.

"What was that," Cristina, who was getting to the table, asked.

"Just a little baseball lingo! You speak English so well I keep forgetting you don't know all our crazy expressions. Now, what should we order?" She smiled at the bemused waiter who handed them the menus. "I can't make head nor tail of it," she eyed the menu and shook her head, crossing her eyes to convey her confusion. "Oh, we Americans and our silly expressions," she said, seeing Cristina had not understood her. "I meant that I cannot understand, so maybe you could order for both of us, Cris. I am easygoing and like mostly everything."

"We will start with their famous *frappé de coco*—very refreshing. Its base is coconut—*coco* in Portuguese," she explained. "When I was a child, I was always told you eat sweets after your meal, but today we will do differently," and she proceeded to order.

The waiter was gone. Desiree, who had remained quiet,

attentively listening to the exchange between Cristina and the waiter, finally voiced her thoughts: "Boy, but this is a beautiful language! I wish I could understand at least a tiny bit," she added. "You Brazilians always sound like you are singing. But not like the Italians—no. Italians sound like they are fighting! And not like the Portuguese from Portugal. Your accent is more...melodious." She tilted her head to one side, and knitted her brows in an effort to find better words. "It is as if you Brazilians glide through the words." She smiled contentedly with her definition. "Now, Robbie, he knows a little Portuguese," and she covertly observed Cristina who, she had noticed, seemed to always pay more attention at the mention of her cousin's name.

"He told me he knows very little."

"Indeed," Desiree answered, thoughtfully. "He did not have the time to learn it; otherwise, I tell you, he'd speak as well as you," she said, nodding. "He will learn anything—if he so decides."

"And what does he do in New York? I mean, work," Cristina tentatively asked.

"He is an engineer." And the beverages having arrived, she proposed a toast: "To a new friendship, may it last for all eternity!" She tried it and opened her eyes wide. "Boy, this is really good."

As the food arrived, Cristina explained: "They don't have formal meals, but mostly finger food. So I hope you don't mind that I ordered an assortment of pastries. I thought you might like to taste some of their specialties." She pointed to each as she named it: "*Bolinho de bacalhau*, which is a cod dumpling; *coxinha*, which is a chicken croquette; and *pastel*, a deep-fried *empanada* generally filled with ground beef. There is a lot of Portuguese influence in Brazilian food."

Desiree was clearly enjoying the selections and the people around them, although she could not understand the conversations, as she had told Cristina.

Suddenly, turning to Cristina, she fired: "Oh, Cris, you're no fun, just like Robbie," she exclaimed with a grimace. "The only time I went out shopping with him—let me see, I think I was fifteen—anyway, it was a complete catastrophe. He huffed and puffed so much I had to give up and turn back home. You are just like him. Why, you won't let me spend the money my husband loves to shower on me, you monster," she mocked a complaint.

Cristina could not help laughing: "As soon as we finish lunch and I go back to work, you can go spend as much money as you want, but, unfortunately, I can't go witness your largesse. Remember: I have to be back at work in time or I'll be in trouble—and you don't want that, do you?"

''Course not, but it would be so much more fun if you could come with me, Cris," she pleaded with a sad expression then continued: "I was barely able to convince Robbie to go with me, but it would be so much easier if you were there and could communicate properly with the natives."

Cristina chuckled. Desiree's face was so expressive; she kept jumping from one subject to the other, matching different facial expressions to each.

"I am sure your cousin will be able to make himself understood. Oh, and before I forget, remember the exchange rate and don't let them take advantage of you," she added.

"Do not fret your li'l head, my sweet! If there is something I am very good at, it is mathematics—especially when it comes to *my* money." And both laughed at her tirade.

The girls chatted away while eating until Cristina realized the time.

"Look at the time—I must rush back to work!"

Desiree accompanied her and they parted at the store's door. She then went in search of Robert, who would meet her at the harbor, where the yacht's launch was docked.

\* \* \*

Later that same afternoon, two men standing on the sidewalk of Carioca Street, in front of Casa Carlos Gomes, attracted mild attention despite the different attire one of them sported; at that time of the year—Carnaval—it was not surprising to see individuals or groups of revelers masked or in disguise at all hours of the day. That was the time of the year where one could be magically transformed into almost anything—Harlequin, Maharaja, Rajah, princess—so a man dressed in colorful Polish garments standing in front of a store was nothing unusual. He was very tall and blond, with a fierce expression on his face, which was increased by his proud posture. The other man was very thin and short, with dark hair and a scant mustache on a mousy face; he was dressed in a white linen pant-suit too big for him. The passersby appreciated the colorful garment of the tall man, not bothering with the short one. Unusual, they might have thought, was the solemn demeanor of that tall *"folião."*[iii]

As Cristina was leaving the Casa Carlos Gomes, the shorter of the two men approached her; his eyes seriously intent on her face, he removed his straw boater hat and saluted respectfully, albeit a bit awkwardly: "My name is Paulo Dias and this is Pawel Symanski. We are here on behalf of our master, Bogdan Zietarski."

Cristina quickly assessed the other young man in the exotic, colorfully embroidered accoutrements, but finding no enlightenment, turned to the one addressing her: "I am sorry, you must have mistaken me for someone else, because I do not know a Bog—anyone of that name."

And as she turned to leave, the tall man planted himself in her way.

"I must explain that my master heard you play a couple of nights ago at the Copacabana Palace," Paulo added quickly. "As the musician who was going to play in tonight's party became suddenly ill, he remembered you and sent me to plead with you to come and play."

She recalled the large man with the fierce eyebrows at Guinle's dinner and concluded that that would be him. She looked to the man in front of her, who had kept silent throughout the exchange, then to Paulo, but said nothing.

"He would be most grateful to you. You see, it would be embarrassing for my master to have nobody performing during the festivities. And he will be very, very generous." As he named a high sum, Cristina could not hide the sparkle in her eyes. Money, Paulo thought, was the Achilles tendon of both men and women…

But Paulo could not know the importance money played in Cristina's life, now that she was the sole provider of her reduced family.

"But in order for me to be able to fulfill your master's request, you need to have a piano."

"We do have one," he quickly added and kept his eyes anxiously on hers.

She bit her lower lip and mentally assessed how much she would be able to accomplish with that amount of money. "Yes," she answered after taking a deep breath. "Just give me one moment to go back inside and get a message to my mother."

She turned on her heels so swiftly neither Paulo nor the other young man was able to stop her. Inside the store she requested the use of the phone and was grudgingly obliged by the manager, who told her not to make a habit of it. When connected with the Copacabana Palace, she asked the telephone operator, a friend of hers, to give her mother a message of her sudden engagement.

Back on the street, and accompanied by the two men, she entered a white limousine and departed to an address somewhere in the Laranjeiras neighborhood.

# CHAPTER 7

As she had mentioned to Cristina, Desiree had a difficult time convincing Robert to accompany her as her interpreter. Max and Spigot promised to join him and share his "doom"—and the word brought an outraged gasp from Desiree. If these two were not able to make the excursion tolerable to him, they at least offered Robert some comic relief. At Ouvidor Street they entered the huge department store *Parc Royal* where they remained for longer than they cared to. Despite making themselves general nuisances, teasing the female clerks and creating all kinds of embarrassing situations, Desiree followed her plan with military precision: she visited all the departments she wanted at leisure, paying little attention to the men's antics. Coming out of the store, they found themselves facing Andrea, who effusively greeted everyone and, inviting himself, merrily joined the party.

On their way back to get to the launch at the harbor, they noticed Cristina entering the back seat of a white limousine, followed by two men. Before disappearing into the car, the taller man took a last look around, as if checking his surroundings. The car slowly started to negotiate its way in the narrow street where horse and hand carts competed with pedestrians and cars, loaded donkeys, and delivery bicycles. The man's furtiveness made Robert uncomfortable. He pointed out the car to Max.

"I am going to follow that limousine, Max," he said, beckoning a taxi cab that abruptly braked in the middle of the street.

"And I am going with you, old chap," Max stated.

At this exchange, Spigot and Andrea, onto whose arms Desiree held, disengaged themselves and set to follow.

"No," before Desiree could open her mouth, Max's voice was stern as he shook his head, "this time you will do as you are told!" He deposited the packages he had been carrying into her unwilling arms and continued: "Take the launch to the yacht."

And before Desiree could react, he gave her a peck on the cheek, turned on his heels, and rushed to the waiting taxi. She remained speechless for a few seconds, exactly where he had left her. Then shrugging her shoulders, turned, and started walking to the harbor.

"Tell Aubrey to come back with the launch and wait for us at the harbor," Robert called after her before entering the cab.

"I'll sit in the front seat, since I can speak Portuguese well enough. *Siga aquele carro*," instructed the driver to follow the limousine that was just turning the corner.

"Well done, *tommy*," Robert patted Max on the back. "That girl is really in need of some control."

"I hate to lose my temper," Max answered, shaking his head in distress, "but sometimes your cousin is a bit trying."

"You're telling *me*," Robert agreed.

"Besides, in her state, she has to settle down now."

"Her state," Robert repeated, confused, but quickly realization dawned on him and a broad smile lit his face. He took Max's hand in both of his and shook it heartily. "Well, Max, so she is. . .you will. . . I mean. . . she will—"

"Yes, Robert, she is and we will," he laughed when he was finally able to extricate his hand from Robert's tight grip.

"And when is the happy day?"

"You know, old boy, I never got around to asking her," was Max's wondering answer.

"Well, it seems the Almighty answered my prayers," Robert said to himself. And turning to Spigot: "Hey, *poilu*, the *tommy* here is going to be a father!"

"Wonderful, wonderful," he exclaimed and gave Max a hearty slap on the shoulder, without losing sight of his quarry.

"Look at him, Max! He thinks we're on a mission," Robert

tried to hide his mounting apprehension with a light remark.

"Robert," Spigot said and suddenly grabbed his lapel and pulled him so suddenly their heads almost collided: "Look, over there, eleven o'clock!" He pointed to the left of their course. "It's their car, I am sure" he exclaimed, excitement thickening his accent. Then, turning a beaming face to Max: "Sorry, I must congratulate you and Desiree more properly when we are back. Some champagne will certainly be appropriate, don't you think?" And giving Max no time to answer, he turned back to where Robert was looking.

In the heavy traffic they could see the white limousine that stood out against the other cars.

"I think you're right, *poilu*," Robert answered, straining his eyes to see the street name they were entering. It read: Leite Leal Street. Learning the name of the street did not help, but if for any reason they had to return to the place, at least he could commit it to memory. And even if he could not correctly pronounce it, he would be able to spell it.

As the limousine turned into a driveway, Andrea instructed the driver to park a little bit ahead. He paid the fare and Robert offered the man a hefty amount if he waited for them. The driver was happily agreeable to the request and, turning the motor off, sunk down in the seat, preparing to wait as long as it took him to win that tempting prize.

"Not many lights and no cars," Max whispered as he and Robert carefully peeked through the gate's iron bars. "Strangely dark and quiet for a party, wouldn't you say so, old boy?"

Robert did not like the look of it and felt anger slowly rising inside him.

"This seems to be a party of two, and I am damned if I don't break a few teeth before the night is over," he growled.

"*Alons, calme-toi!*" Spigot whispered. "You don't know yet if there is anything wrong. The young lady might have been taken to visit some relative..."

"Yeah, sure! A relative sent a white limousine with two odd-looking men to pick her up and visit. Oh, shut up, will you!" Robert took a deep breath. He knew that if he let himself go; if he allowed his feelings to take over, he would lose the calm he needed and maybe jeopardize Cristina, whose situation was unknown. The cooler evening breeze was good and he felt his heartbeat slow down a bit from the rapid pounding of a minute ago. His mind unclouded and he continued to guardedly watch.

He turned to Max and Spigot and, as if in common accord, a service revolver simultaneously appeared in each of their hands. They smiled at each other. "Like old times," he said, while checking the barrel of his. "Sorry, but since you are not armed, maybe you better stay here on watch," he told Andrea.

And the three men watched as he pulled something out of the inside pocket of his jacket. "Meet *la Gioconda, ragazzi*," Andrea said and showed them a Colt .45 with a mother-of-pearl handle and covered with gorgeous engraving. He deposited a kiss on the top of the barrel and fondled it lovingly. "The most beautiful, faithful female I have ever met, this one here."

Raising his eyebrows approvingly, Robert nodded. He, Max and Spigot found a new respect for Andrea. "Well, should we pay these gentlemen a visit?" Robert asked.

The place was very quiet. The only sounds came from the main thoroughfare, Laranjeiras Street, not far from where they stood. Trying to make no noise Robert very slowly pushed the entrance gate open, just enough so they could slip through. And to the other men's complete surprise, he boldly walked to the front door and rang the bell. Max, Spigot and Andrea rushed to join him. The door was opened, and four guns faced the man who appeared framed by the dim background light. He was given no time to even consider a reaction: tucking his gun back into his pocket, Robert jumped at him and seized his throat in a vicious grasp. With the immobilized man, he signaled the others to get in and the door was silently closed.

At a head nod from Robert to Andrea, the latter addressed the man in a whisper in Italian: "*Dov'e la ragazza, stronzo?*"

Robert gave an exasperated sigh and, with gritted teeth, whispered: "In Portuguese, dunce!"

"Oh, sorry. Let's see," and after a couple of seconds' hesitation: "*Onde está a moça, cretino?*"

The man stood obstinately silent. Andrea exhaled an irritated sigh before tucking the Gioconda into his jacket. He amused his companions by pulling a penknife from his pocket and, with a dramatic gesture, flipping it open and pushing the tip to the man's neck. At the touch he gave a muffled gasp. Robert relaxed his grip letting Andrea take charge of the man. "Silence and start moving or I'll bleed you like a pig," Andrea whispered in the man's ear in Portuguese.

No translation was necessary: his companions got the gist of it from the Italian's tone. The man assented with his eyes and started to gingerly move forward across the marble floor of the entry hall, with Andrea's blade still against his neck.

* * *

"You let me go right now and I won't press charges against you!" Cristina's defiant tone hid the horrible fear that was starting to take hold of her.

The man's grin turned into a thunderous laugh. "My little filly, you so amuse me I know I will enjoy your company," he told her in heavily accented English.

Cristina did not know what else to say and could only search the room for a means of escape. She cursed herself for being a naïve idiot—but, again, how could she suspect that in the twentieth century a representative of a Polish prince would plan to abduct her and carry her to the other side of the world like a piece of inanimate luggage?

"Look around as much as you want; you will only leave this house with *me*—and to embark on a long journey." His tone was triumphant. And as he approached her, his eyes translated the desire that burned inside him. "You will love the stud farm, my filly. I can see you riding faster than the wind," and his eyes shone as he spoke.

"I hate farms, can't abide the countryside. And I hate horses more than anything else," she added hastily.

"I will teach you. You will learn to love it all," he said, and suddenly, taking hold of her waist, pulled her tight against his body, trying to kiss her lips.

She fought in vain to free herself. Able to extricate one arm at least, she grabbed a fistful of his abundant mustache, and pulled it with all her might. With a shout he pushed her away.

She stumbled, found support on the wall, and looking back at him, burst into hysterical laughter that she tried unsuccessfully to suppress. More than ever he looked like an enormous walrus. He stood rooted to the spot, his bulging eyes riveted on her, perspiration starting to form on his shaved scalp. Slowly his trembling fingers touched the offended area. Finding blood and a gap where a half of his beloved facial hair should have been, he uttered such a roar that it silenced Cristina's mirth.

"You... You little bitch!" Bogdan Zietarski, manager of the Gumniska stud farm of a Polish prince, was beyond himself with indignation. "How dare you!"

"No, how dare *you*," she cut him fiercely. "You lure me to this house on false pretenses and keep me here against my will! And stop calling me filly, for crying out loud," she snapped back at him, stamping a foot. Then, trying to master her anger, she added on a more subdued tone: "I am sorry, but you tried to take advantage of me and, well, I had to protect myself. But if you let me go now..."

At the furious sparks she saw in his eyes her voice failed her: she read murder in those dark pools. He took a step in her direction, and she felt the blood had frozen in her veins. She closed her eyes, unable to offer any more resistance.

But as he approached her, the door suddenly flew open and of the five people who tumbled into the room, Cristina recognized four: Robert, Spigot, Max and young Paulo. A long minute ticked by while seven pairs of startled eyes observed each other and nothing moved. The static scene was comic, with a very large man with wild eyes, half a mustache, and a bloody patch where the other half should have been. If not for his anxiety, Robert would have erupted in laughter.

As though of common accord, everyone burst into action simultaneously.

Robert ran to Cristina, who—he liked to believe—seemed on the verge of fainting, and caught her in his arms with more passion than a mere rescuer would have been expected to demonstrate. "Are you all right, darling?" he asked, his eyes seeking and finding hers. "If this buffoon did anything, *anything*..." he faltered, "I swear I will kill the damnable brute." His voice was almost inaudible in the background din and confusion. She just nodded and, unthinking, rested her head against his chest. Solicitous, Spigot, Max and Andrea—in that order—ran to their side.

Zietarski's attempt to get to Cristina, first, having been thwarted by Robert's intervening stride, he resumed nursing his offended upper lip, while Paulo, who ran to him, unsuccessfully tried to exculpate himself from the sudden interruption.

"Pawel! Zygmunt! Augustyn!" As Zietarski roared the names of his henchmen, it added to the noise and confusion already reigning in the room. Three colorfully attired young men with alarmed looks jammed through the doorframe—one of whom was known to Cristina: he had helped abduct her—and Zietarski having given an order in Polish, they turned to the rescuers with malevolent grins.

Robert was busy comforting Cristina while his revolver covered Zietarski, behind whom Paulo's small stature was barely perceived. His three friends threw themselves at Zietarski's men and a fist fight ensued. The Poles did not shy from the fight, but Robert's minions, seeming to be hankering for a brawl, decided on a hands-on approach and the guns were not even considered. There was a competition among them to see who could rain down more blows upon their opponents. Broken pieces of furniture flew about; men who were punched and fell backwards immediately charged back; enraged screams and curses abounded in different languages: French, Italian, Polish, and English. To Robert's elated eyes, it was real entertainment, and he cheered and encouraged his team. Cristina, on the other hand, gasped and hid her face on his chest, but took a few peaks and was amazed at Robert finding entertainment in such horrors. Well, that explained men's fondness for boxing, she thought, with an involuntary headshake.

When it all finally ended, the room was a mini battlefield, strewn with broken furniture. Among it all the three young Polish men in different stages of dishevelment, lay moaning or insensible. Robert's friends surrounded him with looks of satisfaction, no less in shambles then their victims, sweaty and panting, but proud of their deeds.

"Not too shabby." Slapping his back Robert teased Spigot, who had been the most ferocious of the three combatants.

"We taught them a lesson," the little Frenchman grinned while trying to put some order to his hair and clothes.

"I think that Polish dog loosened one of my teeth," Max

exclaimed, gingerly trying the injured part.

Andrea looked at Zietarski, who fumed in outrage: his highly skilled men had not withstood the assault of three commoners. "What do we do with the Big Walrus?" he asked, naming an aspect of Zietarski that was in everyone's mind.

"I would think the lady should have the prerogative of this decision," Robert answered, and the others assented.

Cristina turned to Zietarski, whose malevolent eye seemed to cast darts at her. After briefly hesitating she answered, with a mischievous look at him: "Strip them to their underwear and tie them up!"

For a few seconds no sound was heard in the room, but while Zietarski was struck dumb by the proposition, Robert, Spigot, Max, and Andrea broke into riotous laugh.

"*Oh, la bonne idée*," cried Spigot. "And I know where we will find the cords to tie this gang," he said, turning with a triumphant gesture to the curtains that obscured the many windows in the room.

Without a word Andrea extracted his penknife from his bedraggled jacket and went to work.

\* \* \*

The sun had just risen as the young maid started her duties in the kitchen of the house where lodged Bogdan Zietarski. The demanding master required a very large breakfast, which took time to prepare. Suddenly she thought she heard distant rumbling sounds coming from somewhere inside the house. She opened the kitchen door and listened. Silence and darkness met her. But… There it was again, the strange sound. Taking hold of a rolling pin with a somewhat shaky hand, she summoned up the courage to go through the door and advanced into the house on tiptoe. The noises seemed to come from the library. Making the sign of the cross, she slowly pushed the door of that room. As it opened her unoccupied hand flew to seal her lips lest her guffaws would be heard. The scene that met her stunned eyes was one she would never forget, no matter how much longer she lived. It would be told to the other neighborhood maids and provide much entertainment. In the center of the room was a large armchair; tied to it, like a trussed chicken, and in his underwear, was Zietarski, a dark gash with coagulated blood where half of his mustache once grew. On the floor, in the same undressed condition, and tied together in a confused bundle, were little Paulo and the three bulky Polish men; the only difference was that, unlike Zietarski, they had gags over their mouths. The room was in chaotic disorder, strewn with pieces of furniture. One of the curtain panels lay on the floor in shreds, and the silk pulls in all the panels were missing: they had been used to gag and tie them up.

\* \* \*

Following a plan he conceived after his conversation with Ramires, Daniel searched and found a phone number for the person who, he was certain, would help him attain his goal: to possess Cristina. He established contact and secured an appointment and early in the morning took a train to Petrópolis.

Pedro II, Emperor of Brazil, had inherited from his father, Pedro I, a farm by the mountains, where he built the city of Petrópolis. There the wealthy of the city of Rio de Janeiro went to escape summer—and yellow fever. Petrópolis was the official capital of the state of Rio de Janeiro during the First Brazilian Republic, between 1894 and 1902.

Daniel arrived a few hours later, and the crisp mountainous air was a refreshing change from the heat of Rio. His goal was the home of one of the pillars of Petrópolis's society, descendant of an old and respected family, Alexandre Rebelo de Oliveira, whose dwelling he easily found among mansions surrounded by extensive gardens. Upon arrival a wooden-backed butler with a sepulchral face took him to a library decorated with Louis XV furniture. He was offered the traditional *cafezinho*—strong, black coffee, served in a tiny cup—to which he mumbled an acceptance. The steaming beverage, which was left untasted, was soon brought to him, and, after it was served, the butler quietly disappeared. Had Daniel been in a better state of mind, his wondering, vacuous gaze would have certainly admired the leather-bound books lined up on the wall shelves. But he did not have much time to indulge, in his anxious solitude. The door opened and in came his host, Alexandre Rebelo de Oliveira. Daniel sprang to his feet.

Alexandre was a tall man, in early middle-age, but in excellent shape, with an elastic spring to his step that conveyed energy. A wide forehead gave him an intellectual look. Anyone who has seen busts of Caesar would notice the resemblance: the thin face, low eyebrows atop a long nose, and the creases on the sides of the cheeks and thin lips. Like Caesar his grey hair was receding, but unlike that dictator, it was combed back and kept in impeccable order with Brilliantine. Shadowed by the eyebrows, his eyes at first looked black, but as he approached, Daniel recognized the violet hue he knew from another pair of eyes. Yet behind this air of self-assurance and strength was a vacillating and pusillanimous soul.

Immediately, two large young men, one blond with the innocent blue eyes of a cherubim, the other dark with a pair of coal-black eyes, followed him and closed the door. Although so unlike each other, the two were brothers and answered to the names of Castor and Pollux. Gabriel and Mephistopheles, Daniel summed up.

Slowly, the blue-eyed angel walked to the French window while his brother stayed by the door.Not without trepidation Daniel saw the egress from the room blocked.

"Please, sit down, Mr. Cabral," Alexandre invited, after sitting himself.

His voice was deep and the tone was cold, as Daniel had expected. After all, he possessed a pretty damaging secret related to this man's past and did not expect to be greeted with open arms. At a head sign from him, the henchmen left by each of the doors, to stand near enough, Daniel was sure, to return at their master's call.

"Mr. Cabral, it seems you recently came upon knowledge of private information that—if I well recall your words—might be damaging to me if newspapers were to get hold of it." His cold eyes took in the other man's deep blush. "I always prefer to deal quickly with problems, so the question is: what exactly is your goal?" Alexandre's question was as direct as his gaze. He rested his elbows on the arms of the high backed chair and the tips of his slim fingers steepled.

Daniel cleared his throat and tried to show a calm he was far from feeling. He had rehearsed his speech long and hard, but it was not easy to articulate his story, with a pair of stone-cold eyes that seemed to pierce the very depths of his soul, trained on him. But despite addressing this forbidding man, he was able to express himself, he thought, with relative calm.

He told the story he extricated from an inebriated Ramirez. He did not mean to use his knowledge to harm Mr. Rebelo de Oliveira, he explained, but wanted to make sure he understood the seriousness of the situation—at which explanation a cold rictus momentarily twisted Alexandre's lips. Daniel continued: he asked—no, he begged—the only one who could, he was convinced, help him marry the woman he loved. And as this woman was inextricably involved in Rebelo de Oliveira's past, Daniel believed it could incline him to help.

A long silence followed his peroration. And while Alexandre seemed to give the matter thought, small pearls of perspiration started forming at Daniel's forehead. From the man's face nothing could be gaged; it showed no emotion. Only the eyes were alive and, for the briefest of moment, a melancholy expression softened their hardness; but it was gone when he turned them to Daniel.

"For obvious reasons, I conclude you did not share this information with anyone," he more stated than asked, to which Daniel assented, and he continued: "as it would be of no advantage to you. Very well, I have decided to help you," he said, at which Daniel was barely able to suppress a sigh of relief. He continued: "But only under one condition. That as long as you live—and, believe me when I say that I could make it, if not very short, very hard!—you will never again try to get in touch with me. It goes without saying that this is never to be divulged to anyone. Your word as a gentleman will suffice," he said, with a haughty rise of his head.

It was not so much a belief that the other man was a gentleman, but of having made apparent his power to cause Daniel bodily harm that inclined Alexandre to that last statement. The implied threat of Castor and Pollux was more eloquent than any threat he could utter. And at Daniel's solemn promise, he stood up and went to a Louis XV writing table that stood near the French window. Unlocking a drawer, he extricated a folded sheet of paper from a large envelope and went back to his chair.

"Let me tell you a story that, I am sure, you will find illuminating. A few years ago, in my capacity of lawyer, I was helping a lady of my acquaintance. Her husband, who had recently died, had been my client, and I was sorting through his documents when I found this," and he waved the folded paper he had extricated from the writing table. "It is a promissory note." He turned the dangling page to Daniel, who was at a loss as to the document's relevance until he heard: "It is in the name of one Vladmir Abramov."

Daniel's riveted eyes looked for and found the name. He quickly looked at Alexandre, who, refolding the document, continued his narration.

"Abramov was building a house in Copacabana and the enterprise, it seems, was beyond his means. As it happens sometimes to the ones of his class, he wanted to migrate to a higher position in society, and a large house was his way to externalize his—shall we say—*arrival*." A contemptuous grin twisted his lips. "It also seems that *gentleman*"—and he gave the word a contemptuous tone—"was fond of horses... I don't know how he convinced my friend to lend him this considerable amount, but the fact is that he got the money and it was never repaid. That my friend forgot the debt or forgave it is irrelevant. What imports here is that with this document I can avert a scandal." He put the document inside his jacket's breast pocket. "Someone will be in contact with," he hesitated to speak the name, "with the young lady and will explain to her that it is to her advantage to accept you. Were you to renew your proposal, this time, I assure you, it will prove amenable."

Daniel started to express his gratitude, when Alexandre's raised hand cut him short. "There is a condition I make, though. Soon after your marriage, you and your bride will move to another country from whence you will never return." Noticing the other's startled expression, he continued: "All my efforts would be for nothing if her mother could reach her. You must see the logic of my request," he said, to which Daniel was forced to agree. "I will leave to you the details of the trip and the documentation for both of you, but I will advance the necessary funds. Do not thank me," he again interrupted Daniel, "what I do is for my sake and my family's." He turned to the door and called Castor's name. And as the young man's head appeared, Alexandre gave orders: "The gentleman is leaving; accompany him to the door." Castor entered the room and stood behind Daniel. "I bid you good day and good luck," Alexandre said with a cold inflection in his voice, without looking at Daniel.

As the two men exited, Alexandre went to the window and, looking out, saw Joel, his son, playing tennis with one of his many girlfriends. Smart kid, have fun while you can because marriage is no blissful state. Although one could always find rewards in different pastures, he thought, unable to repress a feeling of self-satisfaction. His thoughts veered in a different direction, far away from Rio, to Portugal. More than twenty years ago, was it not, he wondered. What a lovely woman she was; one of the loveliest he had ever met, with that cream-white skin and the hazel eyes. He wondered if she was still beautiful. He had seen the girl from a distance and, even from that far, he saw the stunning resemblance between mother and daughter.

Castor returned to the room with his brother and found Alexandre at the desk. "Early Monday morning you will go to Rio—take the car—and get in touch with the people you and your brother employ for, ah, odd jobs." While talking he scribbled something on a piece of paper and handed it to Castor. "The name is Robert Laughton. Make sure it is just a good beating—d'you hear me?—something that will incapacitate him for a short period. But make sure he will come out of it *alive*." He stressed the last word and his stern look was unmistakable: the brothers knew that no mistake would be tolerated. "I don't want the police involved in this."

He then turned to his address book and, finding what he was looking for, dialed a number.

"Julio, is it you?" he asked when the call was answered. "I am fine, thank you. I am glad you are in Rio because I have a mission for you, and it must be done tomorrow morning." After a short pause he answered: "No, you do not need to come to Petrópolis. It is in Copacabana, not far from your place. Someone will be at your place today with a document. Here is what I need you to do."

\* \* \*

As the train quickly approached overheated, noisy Rio, Daniel felt as if walking on clouds; he was finally going to gratify his most cherished desire. He was certainly not elated at the idea of moving to a foreign country. But the more he pondered, the more he saw at least one great advantage—that of starting a new life in a place where, isolated, Cristina would depend exclusively on him. It was also a sure way to stop the young woman having any more contact with the American. The future looked as bright as the sun he did not see through the train's dusty windows.

\* \* \*

After Robert and his confederates had saved Cristina from the clutches of a loving Zietarski, they went to commemorate their feat. Famished, they landed in a small, downtown restaurant and many toasts were made, one especially for Cristina, who had uprooted part of that gigantic mustache sported by the Polack, the sobriquet Spigot had given to Zietarski. The Frenchman deeply lamented that she had not kept her trophy. It should have been framed for posterity, he told her.

"Pehaps we should go back and reclaim that shpoil of battle?" he asked her, rolling his tongue around the words with some difficulty, his eyes half closed by the amounts of alcohol he had imbibed.

"Let sleeping walruses lie, Spigot," said Robert, to which meaning the addressed remained ignorant.

When they finally dropped her at her home, Cristina tiptoed to bed. Before falling asleep she recalled the scene in the dark entrance hall of her house—she had not dared turn the lights on for fear of being seen. She was lulled into sleep by the image of Robert and slept like a log until Maria—who ignored the prior night's excitement—woke her.

"It's going on ten, young lady. About time you woke up. How was it last night?"

For a second the girl felt tempted to tell her the whole story but dismissed the idea, considering how much it would upset Maria. But also she wanted to avoid the long peroration she knew would follow, with all the details of why respectable young ladies of her class should look for employment—*if* they must—as teachers.

"It went smoothly. They dropped me back home," she lied, shamefully, without a pang of conscience.

"How nice of them. Must have been a very nice dinner party."

"It was." And quite amusing after the initial stressful moments, she thought, and could not help remembering the feeling of resting her cheek against Robert's wide chest—muscular, hard, but so inviting at the same time. She recalled his scent and the beating of his heart, which she could hear despite the terrible ruckus all around them. She wished she could always have that chest to rest her head upon and need not fret or think. . . When they were at her door, he stared into her eyes then flashed a smile that dazzled her. Then came the softest whisper, something that made her heart thump inside her breast: "I love you. Let's have lunch Monday." Before she slowly shut the door, she heard Spigot yell, "Well done!" before being shushed by the others.

She let out a long sigh of contentment and stretched herself, loath to leave the bed where her hazy mind had these events still freshly imprinted. The act of getting up, it seemed to her, would dispel these moments to which her memory held fast. But, she thought, yesterday was as real as today, and the future seemed so marvelous that she could sing. And without realizing it, she started humming a song.

Maria's eyebrows shot up and she gave her a queer look. The girl seemed excessively pleased for merely a successful night's work. "And where was this shindig?" she asked, hiding her suspicion.

Cristina let out a pearl of laughter at Maria's question. "Laranjeiras neighborhood," was the laconic answer.

"And how much did they pay?"

That was a question Cristina had not thought of and so did not have a quick answer. "You know, I don't recall," she said with the air of someone who is making an effort to think, averting her eyes. "I just grabbed the envelope and put it in my pocket. I will look and let you know later."

"Someone you know referred you, I suppose?"

"And you supposed right. It was Mr. Guinle who referred

me to some Polish potentate." And at Maria's confused expression, added: "Someone linked to a Polish prince; I can't recall the name, it was too foreign." She jumped out of bed and started putting on her house coat, hoping to cut the conversation short. God, how she hated lying, she thought.

"Oh, I know someone who will want to write Mr. Guinle to thank him for his kindness..."

"Mother shouldn't do that," Cristina cut in anxiously, and realizing it was the wrong way to approach the matter, changed her tone: "I mean, Mr. Guinle does not like to have people overwhelming him with some syrupy expressions of gratitude. He is a business man. Besides you know mother writes terribly bad in Portuguese."

"Hmmm, what an odd man," she grumbled. "Well, your mother might write bad, but you know I don't, missy!"

"Maria, please don't encourage her by writing for her. I will thank him when I next see him."

Maria thought she smelled a rat, but made no comment. "Well, come have your breakfast and you can tell me all about it."

# CHAPTER 8

After Cristina had fortified herself with breakfast and taken a bath, she and Maria were cleaning the kitchen cupboards when the doorbell rang.

"A gentleman to see you," Maria said after returning to the kitchen. She handed Cristina a business card.

Mystified, the girl read: "Julio Arantes - Attorney at Law."

"I don't know this name… What can he possibly want with me? Are you sure he said he wanted to speak with me, not my mother?"

"He only said he had business with Miss Cristina Abramov," Maria mimicked the man's pompous speech. "The little cake-eater gave me such an appraising look; you should have seen. Perhaps I should go with you?"

"Well, I better see him. What? No," she answered Maria's last comment. "Don't be silly! Take him to the living room while I go to the bedroom to dress in something more appropriate," she said and darted out of the kitchen.

"I lived here almost twenty years, and she suddenly acts as as if I were such a clout that I would slam the door at the man's nose and leave him waiting outside. Humph!"

A few minutes later, Cristina entered the living room. Mr. Arantes leaped to his feet as if propelled by a spring. He was on the wrong side of fifty, short and thickset, and impeccably dressed. His thinning hair was visibly died black, as well as the eyebrows, accentuating his age, which was certainly not the effect he'd had in mind. A white carnation in a silver boutonniere embellished his lapel. Behind his *pince-nez* the eyes of an old *roué*[iv] approvingly admired what he saw. Cristina looked fresh in a very simple cream linen dress with matching shoes. Unaware of the man's expression, she gave him her hand and, sitting on the sofa, motioned him to an armchair.

"Miss Abramov," he started, disregarding the chair and sitting beside her on the sofa, "I have been charged to perform a task that is quite distasteful to me. But," and he sighed deprecatingly, "as I did accept it, discharge it I must, distasteful or not."

If Cristina had been curious when she first handled his card, the man's introduction now mystified her. In silence she waited for him to continue. He fumbled with his briefcase and, without further preliminaries, handed her an envelope.

"I hate to be the bearer of unsavory tidings to such a lovely lady as you are, Miss Abramov." Again, his lascivious eyes approvingly assessed Cristina.

She opened the envelope and started reading the document. Pallor spread over her beautiful face as the contents dawned on her. The hand that grasped the document dropped to her lap while the other stole to her breast. Unable to speak, she stared ahead, unseeing. Here, finally, was the explanation of how her father was able to build their lavish house. Was that why, in his last moments of life, he had begged her forgiveness?

The silence was at length broken by the lawyer's low voice: "You understand that I am not here to, er, collect." And as she frowned uncomprehendingly, he continued: "I was sent to put a proposition to you. If you allow me the impertinence, my age, I should think, puts me in the position of an older brother; and it is as such that I advise you to accept it," he told her, unable to admit, not even to himself, that he was old enough to be her father.

Her eyebrows now shot up. "A proposition? From the lady—"

"No," he cut her short, "not from her, but from my client, who now holds this document—who purchased it, to put it in layman terms—and who shall remain anonymous." By now he was feeling uncomfortable, knowing the blow he was going to deliver to this lovely young lady. He cleared his throat and, fortified, continued: "My client demands no payment in money but proposes a bargain, with the guarantee that this document will remain undisclosed. He proposes that you become engaged and marry Mr. Daniel Cabral. And before you arrive to some erroneous deduction, I can guarantee to you Mr. Cabral is not the holder of this document."

Cristina's surprise and confusion was such that she was momentarily speechless. Marry Daniel? But soon anger aroused her and she gave voice to her indignation: "So this client of yours, *who shall remain anonymous*," she almost spat the words, "sent you to blackmail me! I am to either marry Daniel or my father's memory will be soiled. Why is this person doing this? What possible benefit can be obtained from my sacrifice?"

Her initial outrage had given place to desperation, and the old attorney was loath to perform the cruel task he had been allotted. Yet he was also aware of the fact that Alexandre Rebelo de Oliveira was a very powerful and influential man. So he must discharge this task or reckon with the consequences of failure, which, he knew, could be very disagreeable. Hiding his cowardice behind the thought that, while he could do nothing for the young beauty, he had the right to protect his own skin, he proceeded with his harangue.

"Miss Abramov, you must understand that I am not in a position to pass judgment on anyone, let alone my client. I commiserate with you," to which the girl gave a derisive little snort and turned her head away, "I repeat: I commiserate with you, but I need to make you understand that there is no alternative. I want to make very clear to you that my client will not hesitate to make this document public—*and* demand payment—if you do not agree to an engagement to Mr. Cabral." And as she suddenly looked at the document, he was aware of the girl's thoughts: "I am sorry to have to tell you that this that you hold in your hands is a copy of the original; you can tear it to pieces if you so desire. The original is in the possession of my client."

Clenching her fingers Cristina made the document into a ball, but the source of the horror that had suddenly befallen her life was beyond this mere gesture. She thought furiously but knew that there was no way out. She would never be able to pay that enormous debt yet could not allow her mother to suffer the dishonoring of her father's memory. For a few seconds, Robert's image materialized on her internal retina, but she pushed it away; she refused to expose her humiliation to him. No, he represented a marvelous dream that was to remain just that: something unattainable. No matter how much she struggled, nobody could help her. Quite forlorn of hope, she bent her head to the inevitable. Effacing all traits of her internal struggle, she turned to the lawyer and found a modicum of comfort in the distress she read in his eyes. She tried to get more details, but not more than what he had told could she induce him to say.

"Tell your client I will comply with the bargain. Although by blackmailing me he proves he has no honor, I will trust there is a shred of decency left in your client to compel him to keep his side of the bargain," her last words fell like icicles in the lawyer's ears, so coldly they had been uttered.

In a hazy dream she accompanied the old man to the door and watched him leave. Spent by the effort of maintaining calm, her legs taking her more than her unseeing eyes, Cristina walked to her bedroom. Somehow the light coming from the open window attracted her. Insensible of the beauty of garden and sky on that lovely sunny morning, she leaned against its frame and rested her forehead on the cool wood. No tears fell from her beautiful eyes. She had been stunned near to numbness and had trouble thinking straight. Half an hour passed, and Maria going in search of her, found her in the same position.

"Beautiful day, ain't it?" she asked, surprised at finding the active young woman in a contemplative state.

"Yes." Awakened from her lethargy, Cristina forced a smile. She must keep control of herself at all costs, she thought, and turning to Maria: "I feel a bit tired. I guess I did not sleep as much as I needed. Maybe some coffee will help me." And slipping her arm into the other woman's, directed her towards the kitchen.

* * *

That evening the doorbell rang and Maria went to answer. "Well, well, how spiffy you look, Mr. Cabral. Going to a party?" She stepped aside so he could enter and Daniel smiled nervously.

"And who are the flowers for? No, let me guess," she cut

him short, "they are for Miss Cristina, am I right?"

"Yes, they are. Is she at home?"

"Yes. Go to the living room. I will let her know you are here, and she will join you presently."

The girl changes her mind like the wind, Maria thought. A short while ago, Daniel had been banished like a leprous dog. Suddenly here he is, back, with flowers and that unmistakable twinkle in his eye. What is this girl about, she wondered, and knocked on Cristina's door. "Romeo awaits you, Juliet," she spoke through the closed door and went back to the kitchen.

So the dreaded moment had arrived. Cristina shut her eyes and took two deep breaths. She recalled the phone call she'd gotten from Daniel earlier, warning her of his visit. He had been very specific about the time and made sure she would be ready to see him. There was no mention of the lawyer's visit, but it hung on his unspoken words. Steeling herself, she entered the living room. Daniel sprang to his feet and, extending her a large bouquet of pink roses, started to speak. But she interrupted him.

"Let us not beat about the bush, Daniel." Her voice was frigid and she did not try to veil the contempt in her eyes. The man had become as repugnant as a snake to her, and she had to fight hard to control an impulse to scratch that smile off of his face. "Through a stratagem you are forcing me into a marriage I abhor— much more because of your schemes." He looked at her startled, and she wondered that he expected a different reception. "I am bought and will keep my part of this sordid bargain; I will act accordingly when people are around, but do not expect me to act the same when there are no witnesses." She ungraciously took the flowers from his outstretched hand. "I will give them to Maria to put them in water. When I am back, we will go to my mother and we will enact your little charade."

She turned on her heels and, head held high, was leaving the room when Daniel pulled her back by her arm.

"Not so fast." He surveyed her with unpleasant eyes. "Understand this: the situation has drastically changed." He spoke in icy tones. "Now *I* play the music and you dance—put that into your head. I will not tolerate being slighted by you, do you hear me? And start behaving like the happy affianced young lady you are. Remember that I know all about that little document you were shown today," and he could not help a triumphant feeling as he saw her face blanch at his mention of her father's debt. "Now, my beloved bride, go put the lovely flowers I brought you in the prettiest vase you can find. Then come back and let us go to your mamma to tell her the good tidings!" He let go of her arm, strode to the sofa, and sat down.

Well, it had been easier than he expected, and in time, with him as constant company in a strange country, she would yield to him. She has these grand airs now, he thought, but she will see the futility of struggling. And it seems, Mr. American, that size does not matter; brains do. While you have muscles, I have the brains. And Daniel enjoyed the thought of Robert's reaction to the news of Cristina's engagement.

While she was gone, he made plans to get the marriage license. He also had to arrange tickets on a ship. He would most vehemently avoid New York: it would not do to risk an encounter with the American.

As she carried the flowers to the kitchen, Cristina tried to gain control over her emotions. She was desperately alone; she knew no one could help her and she must accept it. For the sake of her mother, no matter how horrible the future looked, she must at all costs act the part and hide her feelings. She had been allowed a glimpse of a future where love and happiness would be a constant, only to immediately have it all brutally crushed. The catastrophe that had befallen her had to be endured, and she needed to find the fortitude to accept it.

As in a dream she filled a vase with water while Maria prattled nonsensically about her "Romeo." She needed all her self-control not to scream and give way to the wave of desperation that threatened to seize her.

Back in the living room she invited Daniel to the moment she most dreaded, when she would need to play the part of the happy bride to her mother. But she overestimated her powers, for not long after Daniel had left, Maria, seeing her flushed cheeks, touched her forehead and found it hot. The body had succumbed to the excessive stress which the young woman had applied over her psyche.

"You are going to bed, my girl! Yes, and don't you contradict me," she commanded, as Cristina tried to protest, "and I will call Dr. Orlov. With all your budget cuts, it is a wonder to me you did not get rid of the telephone line yet." She tucked the girl in bed and went in search of the doctor's number.

Dr. Anatoly Orlov had escaped Russia in 1916, before the communist takeover. By some fortuitous circumstances, he ended up in Rio and became a great friend of the Abramov family. Being a gourmet—as well as a gourmand—his Sundays were normally dedicated to a somewhat gargantuan lunch, mostly prepared by his own hand. So it was at his post-prandial nap that Maria found him. His housekeeper knowing the doctor's penchant for Cristina, summoned him and he readily answered the phone call. He listened to Maria in silence, as was his habit.

She heard his thunderous bass voice: "I will see the girl. Do not fret, I will be there soon," he said in heavily-accented Portuguese and hung up without saying goodbye—another of his habits, and one that drove Maria to distraction. Every time she had tried to beat him to it, she was defeated. Curse the man, she thought, and slammed the phone in an impotent gesture.

* * *

After he examined Cristina Dr. Orlov told Maria: "Girl is healthy, nothing wrong with the body. Problem is here," and he tapped a fingertip to his forehead. "Something stressed her much, so the body rebelled and fever resulted." His ponderous shoulders shook as his hands were thrown around in a gesture of helplessness. "Keep her cool, give her light food and *no—no* stress, *no* excitement, you hear?" And he looked at Maria with such severity, his eyebrows joined in such an ominous frown, the poor woman felt that, somehow, she was the cause of Cristina's troubles. "Mrs. Abramov is well? She needs me?"

"No, she is having an exceptionally good day and does not know yet that Cristina is not feeling well." And running after the doctor as he made his way to the front door, she reminded him: "Please, remember to send your bill, doctor."

"No bill, no bill to friends," he boomed at her, waving his hands scandalized at the idea, and without even turning to her, left, banging the door behind him.

"This darn Russian bear always gets the better of me," the

disgruntled Maria mumbled. "Well, at least there will be no bill," she told herself cheerfully.

\* \* \*

Monday at noon, an anxious, but happy, Robert showed up at Casa Carlos Gomes.

"Miss Abramov called this morning to inform us she no longer works here. Very thoughtful of her, I must say. I wonder what that young lady plans to live on." Like most people when conversing with a foreigner, the manager spoke loudly and pronounced his words slowly. His tone left no doubt that he was far from pleased. "Probably found some rich man to pay her bills," he added, giving Robert a meaningful look, which he quickly regretted, seeing the dangerous flash in the young man's eyes.

Robert controlled himself enough to avoid punching the man. After his questions were answered, he was still unable to learn more about Cristina's surprising decision. He left the place and caught a cab, giving Cristina's address to the driver. He could not know that Maria had been instructed by an extremely anxious Cristina that under no circumstances should Robert know she was at home. Maria was to tell him she had travelled to see a sick relative and did not know when she would be back.

"Well, I never! Be forced to lie to people and without even knowing if there is a good reason for the lie," she remonstrated with the girl.

"Please, Maria, I *do* have a very good reason. Have I ever given you reason to doubt me?"

"Plenty," was the outraged answer. "But I will do as you wish. God only knows what machinations are afoot." And after checking Cristina's temperature, gave her a disapproving look and left with a displeased harrumph.

And so it was that Robert was met with this startling information and, try as he did, he could not find out more. Stunned, he had no recourse but to leave. He strolled aimlessly through Atlântica Avenue, thinking he might see something that could help elucidate the mystery of this sudden trip. As nothing happened, and since his launch was moored at the harbor downtown, he took a tram back there. While the tram took him through sceneries he did not see, he tried to sort things out, and decided it would be best to send his father a telegram. Upon arriving downtown, he quickly directed his steps to the building of the *Correios e Telégrafos*, at *Praça XV de Novembro*, or XV of November Square.

Built in 1743 the premises of the post office had been used for various purposes throughout the history of the city. Originally the Governor's House, it became the *Casa da Moeda* and the *Real Armazém*, respectively—the Mint and the Royal Warehouse. In 1763 it was turned into the *Paço dos Vice-Reis*, the Palace of the Viceroys. When escaping Napoleon in 1808, the Portuguese king, Dom João VI, made it the *Paço Real*, the Royal Palace. In 1822 his son, Pedro II, having become emperor after declaring the Brazilian independence from Portugal, named it the *Paço Imperial*, or the Imperial Palace. It was from one of its rooms that, on May 13th 1888, Princess Isabel, daughter of Dom Pedro II, signed a law freeing the slaves. And from this building, in 1889, on a hot November night, the last Braganza, the sexagenarian Pedro II, left Brazil deposed by the Military. Unfortunately, this example of Portuguese colonial architecture had been "modernized" and had lost its original charm. The much-altered building became the post office that Robert entered: the *Agência Central dos Correios e Telégrafos*.

Inside the building he found a modicum of respite from the pitiless heat. At the counter he addressed a young man wearing a highly starched collar with bowtie who seemed oblivious of the oppressing heat and humidity. "*Telegrama, por favor*," he said, fanning himself with this hat.

With a nod, the teller handed him a pencil and a form on which Robert wrote the following:

*Send countess to Rio urgent. Ship from Munson Steamship Lines. Confirm departure.*

"Nova Iorque. Urgente," he explained as he handed the young man the urgent message to be telegraphed to New York.

The clerk, who understood English enough, was duly impressed by this foreigner's dealings with a countess and made sure the important message was sent with all due haste. Back in New York, his father read the telegram and chuckled. But, he thought, how did the boy guess who his friend was? Well, somehow he did, the smart puppy!

As he left the Post Office building, Robert walked aimlessly for a while, still pondering on the latest startling developments concerning Cristina. He was baffled by her sudden decision to quit a job that, he knew, was monetarily important to her. Something really momentous must have happened to force Cristina to that action, that much was obvious. He had the tale of the trip to some unnamed relative from the lips of Eugênio's sweetheart, Maria. Yet, it sounded just like that: a tale. He thought Maria seemed uncomfortable while talking with him, and it was not solely from the effort of making herself understood and grasping his halting words.

A growl from his stomach reminded him that breakfast had been a long time ago. He checked his watch. He had not realized it was so late. The intense heat brought to his mind the Brazilian *chope*: a glass of beer. As he looked around, trying to get his bearings, he noticed that he was standing in front of what looked like a small bar. He read the sign: *Bar Adolph*. He entered and, despite the lateness of the hour, was able to get something to eat, what Brazilians call "*aperitivos*"—little hors-d'oeuvres. Ravenous, he gobbled it all down quickly, while enjoying the refreshing beverage. Satiated, he had to control himself not to echo his neighbor's loud burp.

When Robert finally left, it was late afternoon. Had he been paying attention to his surroundings he would have noticed two men who had been shadowing him for some time. He walked out of the Iron Arm from 105 Assembleia Street, turned left into Rua do Carmo and, absorbed in his thoughts, entered the narrow Beco dos Barbeiros.[v] Looking ahead of him he noticed that thoroughfare ended in another street, not in the wide Praça XV de Novembro, or XV November Square, that faced the harbor. Fearing he might get lost, he turned back to retrace his steps when two burly men barred his way, arms akimbo, donning unfriendly faces. They were tall and the tight jackets they wore only emphasized that they were both of muscular build.

"Hey, fellas," Robert flashed a wide smile at them. "I think the three of us can comfortably walk abreast through this street. Nice meeting you." The men's expression told a not so nice tale. As Robert tried to pass them, the one nearest to him, the tallest, a nasty looking individual with a boxer's nose and cauliflower ears, stepped in his path. Shoving his right hand down his pants pocket Robert grabbed some coins and showed a hand full of coins. "What, calling for an unpaid bill?"

He thanked his Guardian Angel for having put a New York street thug in his life: Bunky Griffith, who had taught him defensive moves since childhood. Quickly rolling the coins into a stack in his clenched fist, he braced himself for the inevitable. "Look, I just want to go home." Suddenly he looked at the shoes of the huge ogre in front of him and said: "Now, *where* did you get those wonderful shoes?"

As the man looked down, Robert quickly reared back and with the fist enclosing the roll of coins, swung at the man's jaw with all his might. One thug down, he mused. But before he could finish that thought, the other man punched him in the cheek, sending him to the pavement, and started kicking him in the ribs. Robert doubled over in pain and to protect himself. Suddenly, as if by magic, a man came silently out of the shadows, running. He came to a stop and placing both hands on the pavement, raised his torso in the air, and with one foot dealt Robert's assailant a powerful kick on the back. The thug was sent railing against the wall, where he bounced and fell to the floor like an emptied sack of potatoes: his opponent was hors de combat!

Meanwhile Robert was able to stand up and rested his left shoulder against the wall, holding his right arm. Even in deep pain as he was, he marveled at the young man's agility. His movements were as light as a ballerina's. His body had pirouetted in the air with the lightness of a feather. He had never seen movements such as those, so supple.

"Watch out!"

Robert's warning came out too late: as Robert's savior was straitening himself up, the thug who had been lying on the pavement got up and, coming from behind, grabbed him by the neck. The young man grabbed the hem of his attacker's trousers. With a quick jerk he pulled the man's feet off the ground, and, with the thug still holding his neck, he threw himself backwards, falling with all his weight on top of his attacker. The thug was stunned by the shock and his arms immediately relaxed.

The young man straightened himself up, pulled a handkerchief from his pocket and cleaned his hands. He then went to Robert and gingerly turning the other's face with deft fingers, examined the damage.

"Tsk, tsk, tsk," he clicked his tongue and shook his head in commiseration. "This one will leave a small scar," he pointed a finger at Robert's cheek. Then he smiled: "Still, females love a pretty scarred face. Anything hurt here?" he asked, patting Robert's ribs.

Robert, who understood enough of what was said, winced, but shook his head, and motioned to his right arm. The young man deftly removed his belt and passing it around the back of Robert's neck, made it into a sling. "Better?'

The answer was a nod. "Launch . . . Harbor . . ." With an effort Robert was able to pronounce these halting words in Portuguese. "Take me . . . to yacht," and he could say no more.

"Lean on me." The young man put Robert's left arm across his shoulder, and started to half walk, half drag him out of the street. "I'll take you to your boat, but first we are going to a doctor," and he cut Robert, who had understood the last word, "you need attending to. Dr. Menezes is right at the corner and he will do a marvelous job patching you up." He smiled, for he could see Robert had only half understood his reasoning.

Dr. Aldo Menezes was still in his office. Mrs. Menezes, the receptionist cum nurse, a big bosomed red-haired lady, was thrilled when she learned that Robert, like her, was from New York. "Well, my family is actually from Ohio, but we have lived so long in New York," Robert explained.

Dr. Menezes was Brazilian but had lived many years in New York, where he met and married his wife Mary. He was her opposite: short, thin, with coal-black hair.

"Shoulder dislocation," he told his wife, who nodded her head in agreement. "Well, lucky for you, young buck, I've have treated many similar cases—and from similar causes too." Expressing himself in very good English, he deftly and quickly attended to Robert's shoulder. Praising the young man's stoic silence to what he knew was a painful procedure, he applied a little piece of folded gauze to the small cut on his cheek and covered it with adhesive tape. "I wish we had available this new product from the States—what is it called again, Mary?"

"Band-Aid," was the answer.

"Yes. It seems it is ready to use, a real marvel. Here's another," he winked and handed Robert a snifter of brandy. "Now, loose it down the hatch. It is a treatment I find helpful in many cases—although only the special ones get my favorite brandy."

"You'll get no complaint from me, doc." Robert forced a smile. The pain had been almost unbearable and his greatest fear was that he would swoon like a girl!

"As we were all upset by this violence perpetrated against you," Dr. Menezes continued, "I will recommend the treatment to the whole company, myself included." He served three more glasses, then raised his: "Your very good health, Mrs. Menezes, and long life to both of you, young men." He then took a long drought, smacking his lips. And turning to Robert: "I found no other injuries. But make sure you give at least couple of weeks before you get into another street brawl, young man. Keep this arm in the sling. And *take it easy*," he stressed the words, poking Robert's chest with a thin forefinger.

When Robert tried to pay the office visit, Mary Menezes shook her head: "Get outta here, boy! It is not often I have the pleasure of helping my husband mend a countryman! Here," she handed him a card with their address. "In case you need to send someone to fetch my Aldo. We live right on top of the office." And with a friendly pat at Robert's cheek, shooed the two young men to the street.

It was a short walk to the harbor—although rather painful for Robert—where his savior helped him into the launch. He pointed to a yacht that stood to their right, about a quarter mile away. The young man steered the launch and in a few minutes they were boarding the yacht.

"What on earth," Max exclaimed seeing Robert dragged into the deck by a stranger. "Did you get run over by a train?"

"You should have seen the other guy," was Robert's answer. As he smiled the little nick on his upper lip opened and let a few of droplets of blood, which he licked.

"Here, let's take him to his cabin," Max addressed the young man.

"Slow down or he won't understand you, Max," Robert explained.

But the young man told them in broken English that he did

speak a little bit—very, very little, he explained with the help of thumb and forefinger: a tiny gap between these two digits showed the extent of his understanding of that language. And he smiled broadly, exposing dazzling white teeth that seem to gleam against his ebony skin.

Bunky intercepted them halfway down the steps and took over Max's side.

"Look at ya! Looks like you've got ran over by a train. Will you ever stop giving us cause for anxiety, Master Robert?"

Robert screwed his face at him, but refrained from answering.

As Bunky and the young Brazilian laid Robert in bed, Desiree burst into the room like a tornado. "I was told you had a little accident while—" and she cut her sentence short. "Oh, my God, Robbie, what happened," she screamed and lunged in his direction—an action that was deftly intercepted by her husband.

"Calm down, old girl, he is fine now," he told her.

"But look at his face... Look and his arm...," she continued in loud tones. And with a disgusted look: "Your clothes, your beautiful linen suit, your shoes, it is all ruined," she shrieked.

"Stop this screeching, for Pete's sake," Robert grunted, while Bunky motherly arranged the pillows behind him. "You sound like a wailing ambulance siren! All this screaming is giving me a headache. Besides, you should know that women in your condition must be more careful, more sedate. . ."

"Women in my con—well, I never! Maximilian, you beastly creature, you told him!" With a frown she folded her arms in front of her and gave her cringing husband a withering look. "Snake," were her sibilant words to her spouse before she turned her attention back to Robert. "What really happened to you? Looks like you got run over by a train," and she held her hand to his face, but he pushed it away.

"Nothing that dramatic, oh, theatrical cousin of mine," at which comment she did her regular sticking out of a pink tongue at him. "I think I exceeded my beer quota: I slipped on the uneven pavement and fell. This gentleman kindly took me to the local medico and, well, here I am—and here he is." And turning to the young man: "I don't even know your name," he said in halting Portuguese.

"Antonio Laurindo das Neves, at your service," he said, and, for the benefit of the assembled company, he flashed that easy bright smile Robert had already experienced.

"I am Robert—as you might have already learned," at which words the young man nodded. "I don't know how to repay your help except by thanking you yet again," Robert said with a shrug of the shoulders. Then turning to his cousin's husband: "Max, would you be so kind and ask Eugênio to come over to help me?" And as the Englishman went to the kitchen searching for the chef, he explained: "He is Brazilian and will be able to translate."

Antonio agreed with a head shake.

Robert noticed Desiree gazing at the young Brazilian. "You seem to like my friend. Considering his name for the brat?"

She gave him a severe look. "Most certainly, although it's none of your business. But I was actually thinking that I would love to sketch this young Brazilian's face..."

Bunky having unsuccessfully repressed a chuckle and receiving a withering look from the lady, quietly removed his bulk from the room.

"You? Sketch? Now, *that*'s rich." He burst out laughing, which sent a sharp stab of pain to his lacerated lip. "You can't even hold a pencil," he grumbled, holding a finger against the injured part.

"You always talk about my taking some useful occupation. Well, when an excellent opportunity presents itself what do you do? Put me down! Thank you very much!"

During this exchange the young Brazilian looked from one to the other with a puzzled expression.

"You will have plenty of occupation when this brat hatches," was Robert's ungracious comment.

Desiree was unable to retort with the arrival of Max and Eugenio; the latter having greeted Antonio—who he apparently knew—enquired about Robert's health.

"Now, here, Robbie, I want to know the truth, not some tale of you slipping on the sidewalk. I'm not a child! I won't leave this room until you tell the real story," and Desiree sat by the bedside, giving it such a shake that Robert sat up, and grunted, in pain. "Unless you *did* get run over by a train..." And she fluttered her eyelashes at him.

"Just so I can quickly have a view of the back of your head, I'll tell, but I don't even know what it was about. I was returning to the launch when these two toughs came out of nowhere. I got one down, when the other caught me as I was turning to him. I reeled and hit my shoulder against the curb. He was trying to finish the job—most likely with a good kick to my poor ribs—when Antonio here showed up." He looked at the young Brazilian, then turning to his cousin's husband: "Max, you should have been there to see this guy fight!"

"No, he shouldn't, and I thank God he wasn't," Desiree protested.

Ignoring her comment, Robert went on to describe his savior's moves in detail. Max marveled at the tale. Suddenly Spigot erupted into the room.

"*Nom d'un nom*! But what happened? A train drove over you?"

Robert gave a low groan and looked pleadingly at his friend: "Et tu, Brute?"

Spigot disregarded the comment. "I heard you're beaten up pretty badly—to a pulp, it was the term, I think. I see it is true. Could not take one opponent, hein?"

"Oh, sit down and shut up, Spigot. I can only take one Desiree at a time."

"Well, this male gathering is starting to get to my nerves. So much so," and Desiree made a face, "that right now, even the company of your friend Sarah sounds alluring." And with this she left.

"Eugenio, I must know where this guy learned how to fight!"

"It is called Capoeira, Sir. It is a dance-fight inherited from the African slaves. Antonio learned it as a child, from an expert: Mr. Ciríaco Francisco da Silva, whose sobriquet is *Macaco*—'monkey' in English," he explained. "Capoeira is actually criminalized and, when caught, the *capoeiristas*—that is how they are called—get jail time or worse."

"Is it restricted to people of African descent or can a white dude like me learn it? Or am I too old?"

After briefly conferring with his friend, Eugênio explained that Antonio would be happy to introduce Robert to his teacher,

*Mestre Macaco*. Robert looked young and very fit, so Antonio thought he could certainly learn. As Robert was not sure how much longer they would stay in Brazil, and, worse, how long he was to be immobilized, it was decided that he would be in touch with Antonio at the address he was given. He assured the young man that if he had to leave soon, the next time he was in Brazil he would make time to learn Capoeira. (When later on she was told, Desiree concluded that this would be a returning trip that could only have Cristina as the reason—great tidings to her mind bent on matrimony.) After wholeheartedly thanking the young Brazilian— to whose pocket had been added several crackling dollar bills—he asked Eugênio to see that the young man would be taken to the shore by Audrey. "And, please, select a bottle of my brandy and ask Antonio if he would not mind dropping it at Dr. Menezes's with my compliments."

Alone with Spigot, Max and Bunky, who had slipped in as soon as Desiree had left, Robert succinctly told them of Cristina quitting her job and her purported absence from home to take care of an enigmatic relative. His two chums agreed that something was wrong, but neither had an explanation.

"I wonder if The Polack again kidnapped Mademoiselle Cristina." To Spigot, Bogdan Zietarski would forever be "The Polack." Robert argued that, if that were the case, Maria would have been frantic and would have definitely told him.

"Sounds more like these two guys were torpedoes," chimed in Bunky.

"And who the hell do you think would want to kill me here in Rio, Bunky? Very few people know me," was Robert's annoyed response.

"Goes to show what baggage you are: just arrived here and people already trying to blip you off!" The comment went completely ignored by Robert.

The next morning Bunky came into Robert's room with a breakfast tray, which he unceremoniously put on the bed beside him.

"My dear man, you have the light touch of a loving nanny," said Robert, with a candid smile at Bunky, who looked back with a forbidding expression. "Do I detect censure in your generally loving eyes? What ails you, nanny?"

"Now, that's exactly it: me here acting as your nanny. That could have been prevented if you didn't venture out all by yourself to be beaten by some hitmen."

Robert remained untouched by this criticism. "*Che sarà, sarà*, as our friend Andrea would tell you."

"Yeah, you get into trouble and I have to bring you food in bed, as if I had nothing better to do in life! Need me to spoon-feed you or are you strong enough to do it yourself?" And then, pulling an envelope from his pocket, a bright smile spread his mustache and he waved it at Robert with a large paw. "Telegram from daddy," and he dropped it in the young man's lap.

Robert eyed the opened envelope and handed it back to him: "Since you already broke into my private correspondence, read it while I eat."

Unfolding the inside paper Bunky cleared his throat and read it with a solemn expression: "Arriving eleven days from receipt of this with countess. Love, father. " After a brief pause, he continued: "PS: Bringing new wife. Met her in local burlesque. Her name is Boopsey. I call her Bubbles. You can call her mom. Ain't that lovely?" Dropping the telegram on the bed he pursed his lips and contemplated his hands. He then gave Robert a droll look.

For a man of Bunky's size, he displayed extreme agility at avoiding the glass of ice water Robert had thrown at him. He sneaked his head back in and left the young man with a parting comment: "I don't know, but this love of yours has damaged your aim."

# CHAPTER 9

For the next several days, after Max talked Robert into it, he and Spigot kept a discreet surveillance on Cristina's house. Together or separately, they made their headquarters on the front terrace of the Copacabana Palace, that commanded a good enough view of Cristina's house; with Spigot's binoculars they could easily identify anyone arriving or leaving. A cool drink in hand, they enjoyed the sea breeze, but with the sun on its zenith, there was no remedy but to ignore the sweat drenching their clothes.

One evening Max, accompanied by Spigot, came into Robert's room. They had decided it was time to give the young man the news, which was not very encouraging. "Well, old boy, it seems to us there is something going on in that house," to which Spigot agreed. "And Eugênio visited his friend, Miss Maria, a couple of times, he told me, and each time she was reticent and too eager to get rid of him."

"I understand exactly what you mean, Max. Maria did not seem very communicative when last I saw her."

"Also," Max said, "Spigot and I saw a man go into the house on several occasions." And Max went on to describe Daniel. "During that time no one else went in..."

Robert noticed his hesitation. "Anything else?"

Max looked at Spigot who took the cue and, unwillingly, added: "Afterwards the same man came out with Miss Cristina. And they went for a stroll..."

And as Robert did not say anything, Max added: "We noticed the young lady did not seem very willing. It seemed she was *led*, if you know what I mean.'

Robert nodded in agreement. "Yes, and I think I know who the man is," he said after a few seconds of embarrassing silence, and his lips set on a grim line. He recalled Daniel described in Ramires' reports. So, there was a romantic interest on the man's part, he concluded to himself. And at that thought his hands clenched into tight fists, until the knuckles went white.

Max noticed this and knew that it did not brook well for the other man.

Max and Spigot eyed each other. "Does sound a bit rum, old boy," the Englishman ventured. Then turning to Robert: "I say, what if Spigot and I continue the watch on the place?"

Robert shook his head: "I don't think you'd learn anything else, Max." He was pensive for a few minutes, and then his thoughtful eyes met Max's. "I guess I might have to pay the lady a visit." And before the other two could voice dissent, added: "This is my problem and I've already involved too many people trying to figure things out. I need some time alone to think and decide what I must do."

"Which means: you'll do what you want in the end. You are being a complete dunce, as always." And at that, he and Spigot retired, leaving Robert in a brown study.

Max went in search of his wife, wondering what new misdeeds she might be concocting. Spigot sauntered to the kitchen, to see what new marvels Eugênio was concocting.

The following morning, after several days fidgeting from bed to chair and vice-versa, and outbursts of temper—the latter caused by Desiree's repeated teasing—Robert's forbearance had reached its limit. He jumped out of bed, had a quick breakfast and a shower and decided he would go in search of news from Cristina. Risking a peak in Spigot's quarters he found it empty and got a hold of his friend's binoculars. He successfully escaped Bunky's vigilance, but as he reached the deck he found Spigot and Max who feigned surprise at seeing him there.

"Well, good morning! Come to take the morning air with us, old boy," Max asked and seeing the binoculars, added: "or birdwatching?"

He scowled at both men. This has Bunky's hand all over it or my name is not Robert, he thought, and directed his steps to the launch, having told Aubrey he would not need him to get to shore, that he would do it himself.

Without asking, Spigot and Max jumped in. "We're going, too, *mon petit*," the former told him incisively.

"So long as you both stay out of my way," Robert yelled above the engine's noise.

"Of course you won't need us," said Max shrugging his shoulders and, pointing at his arm sling: "because this won't hinder your movements, of course."

Robert ignored his two friends while they prattled in the background, keeping his own council. Half hour after leaving the yacht, a taxi deposited them in front of the Copacabana Palace. They went up to the front terrace, the same place where Spigot and Max had paced and watched for days in a row. The minutes dragged and they had a hard time holding Robert.

"It is too early in the morning for a visit, Robert," Max argued.

"And they might have gone to the mess, you know, the church," Spigot chimed in.

A car passing in front of the hotel, stopped at Cristina's front door and a man emerged from it.

"Hey," Robert protested as Spigot grabbed his binoculars.

"It is that man I saw here before," the Frenchman told Max. "The same one you saw too, Max. Regard," and he tried to pass the binoculars to Max, but Robert was faster.

He cursed under his breath as he looked through the lenses. "You two stay right here," Robert commanded, shoved the binoculars into Spigot's hands, and left quickly.

Through the lenses Spigot watched Robert dart down Atlântica Avenue toward Cristina's house.

"What's happening?" asked an anxious Max.

"He is ringing the. . .how do you say—*la sonnette*?"

"Doorbell, you stupid Frog," Max yelled. "What else?" And, impatient, forced the lenses out of Spigot's tight grip.

"*Ah, mais ça, alors!* What's happening? Tell me this moment!"

"He's going in…" A few seconds elapsed before he

continued: "He's not exactly *going* in: he is forcing his way in. I think we should follow him, Frog."

The two exchanged a quick, troubled glance and careered out of the building.

* * *

Maria answered the door. Robert stood there, looking at her with a serious countenance, his left arm hanging on a sling. Curse the girl, she thought aware of the embarrassing position she had been forced into by Cristina. She had been coerced to lie to Robert once, then to Eugênio on a couple of occasions; she had told Cristina that that was it, there would be no more lies! Yet, after looking at his face, she flashed a nervous smile and told Robert Cristina was not home.

"And the gentleman who just got in: who is he visiting? Her mother?"

"Yes, yes, her mother." The answer came too fast. "Well, I am sorry, but I am very busy in the kitchen, Sir. I will let her know you came by." And as she started to shut the door he blocked it with his foot.

"I'm sure you won't mind if I wait for her inside. It is very hot out here."

"But I don't know what time she will be back," she said as he pushed the door open and made his way in.

Suddenly, behind Maria, Cristina appeared, followed by Daniel.

"Robert," she uttered in a half-smothered exclamation. "What is wrong with your arm?" She ran to him, but stopped short. Yet her eyes could not hide the joy of being near him after so many days of a forced separation. All the things she would like to say to him—how she missed him, the almost physical pain of the separation—were caught in her throat and almost chocked her. His eyes caressed hers softly. She took a deep breath and closed her eyes a mere instant. Her body slightly swayed and she was caught by Robert's left arm. When she opened her eyes, she saw his troubled ones looking down at her.

That simple gesture—the look in his eyes—she thought, had more love in them than Daniel would ever feel or even understand in the whole of his life. This was what she had to give up—and for what, she asked herself, bitterly. To keep intact the honor of a father who had gambled on horses and lost; whose ridiculous dreams of grandeur had landed her in the hands of one such as Daniel! He was dead now, gone, she reminded herself, so why not just chuck it all out? Why not let herself go and fall into this man's arms—this man whose eyes screamed his love for her? As the image of her mother materialized in her mind, she knew she would rather sacrifice herself than subject her to the knowledge of her beloved husband's faults. Her mother would never recover from that shock.

All this she thought in the few seconds, while she momentarily rested against Robert's chest before she looked up and their eyes locked in silent dialogue.

"What is this, Cristina? Get away from this man, I'm telling you," Daniel shrieked. "Get away from him or suffer the consequences!"

Holding her firmly against his chest, Robert ignored Daniel and pleaded with Cristina: "Come with me, my darling, please," and he started to slowly walk towards the door, gently guiding her along with him.

"I can't," she whispered and, reluctantly, freed herself from his embrace.

Robert, who had continued walking, had just walked out the front door when Cristina was suddenly catapulted pass him and fell on the landing as the door was slammed shut after her. At that moment Max and Spigot arrived. They quickly kneeled beside her and helped her up.

"You swine," Robert roared. He tried the door but it was locked. He then backed up and, gaining momentum, slammed against the door with his shoulder. It flew open and he rushed in. Seeing him Daniel started to run, but Robert was faster and grabbed him by the collar. Unfortunately for Daniel, the chase ended inside the powder room. Robert grabbed Daniel's head and shoved it inside the toilet bowl while Spigot and Max tried to stop him.

"You're going to drown him, Robert!" Max tried to reason with him. "Are you mad?"

Finally, having had enough, Robert pulled the man's head

out of the toilet bowl and, shaking him like a ragdoll, yelled, his face an inch from the other's: "Don't you ever touch her, you hear me, you scumbag!"

Carrying the disheveled man by his collar, he went back through the corridor, where he passed a horrified Cristina; Maria had joined Sonya in the garden and was glad the older woman had heard nothing.

"Please, Robert, stop," Cristina pleaded.

"I am going to throw this trash where it belongs: in the street."

"No, please, don't do that," and turning to Max with a pleading expression: "Can't you do something to stop him?"

Max shook his head, despondently. "Sorry, but he won't listen to me." And noticing her look at Spigot, he added: "And especially not to him."

Robert walked back inside the house and explained: "I put him in his car and told him to go home." He looked at Cristina. "Now, you and I are going to have a talk, my girl."

"No, we are not," she almost screamed and yanked away the hand he had caught in his. "You have done enough for one day. Look at this door," and she pointed at the broken frame.

"This is not a problem, I will have it fixed. But we need to talk. I'll give you a choice of places: inside or outside."

"Neither," she shook her head looking at him with eyes she willed cold. And as he tried to take hold of her hand to pull her out of the house: "Robert, listen to me: I am engaged to be married to Daniel."

The silence that followed seemed to her to have lasted an eternity. Robert's amazement was so complete that, for a moment or two, he could find no words with which to express it. And when his voice was finally heard, it was rasping and low: "Engaged? To that sewer rat?"

"What you think of him is irrelevant. The fact is that we are engaged. You had no right to force your way into my house and commit that violence against my…" She hesitated, for there was a bitter taste to the word: "fiancé! Please, please," she pleaded in a desperate tone, "go away." Then, turning to his friends: "Please, take him away." She crossed her arms in front of her chest and turned her back to him; she had reached her limit and could not trust herself to witness Robert leaving.

As the damaged door was clumsily shut behind them, she slowly crumpled to the floor, where Maria found her a few minutes later.

"What is it, my pet? What is happening? Can't you confide in me as you always do, my dear?"

Cristina burst into tears. She wept passionately, almost hysterically, and buried her face against the other woman's shoulder. Maria was at the point of weeping herself, so intense was the girl's distress. But controlling herself she gently pulled Cristina to her feet and took her to her bedroom, where she helped the girl into the bed. After a few minutes the tears stopped and Cristina lay very quiet.

"I will make some passion flower juice for you, to calm you down, my dear," Maria told her.

"No, please, stay," said Cristina, and, holding the woman's hand, pulled her back to her side. "This is killing me, Maria, I *need* to confide in someone or I will choke—and it must be you, the only one I can trust with this secret." She took a deep breath and willed back the tears that were beginning to fill her eyes. She told Maria what the visit of the pompous little man, Julio Arantes, had meant.

Outraged, Maria cursed the memory of the lawyer, of Daniel, and of the person—whomever it was—that held the promissory note. "My dear, you cannot sacrifice your entire life for this. Your mother will understand, I promise you."

"You know it would be the death of her. She idolized father—you know that—and this would kill her." Feverishly, she held the woman's hands in a tight grasp: "Promise me that you will not breathe a word of this to my mother." Then added hastily: "Or to Robert—or his friends. Promise!"

In the end Maria had to promise, for the girl was working herself into a frenzied state. And as she was leaving the bedroom, the outrage perpetrated against her darling almost choked her. Then she realized she had not promised not to tell Eugenio. He might think of something. Desperate for help, she felt a modicum of relief at the thought.

* * *

As in a dream, Robert allowed his friends to lead him away from Cristina's house. They walked to the Copacabana Palace and directed their steps to the bar.

"Right now you need a good snort of whiskey, old man," and Max ordered the drink.

Only after taking a few sips of it, Robert seemed to wake up to his surroundings. He looked around, and then noticed his friends' anxious expressions.

"Are you all right?" Max asked.

"Oh, I'm still a little shaken, but I will be fine soon," answered Spigot.

"I'm talking to Robert, idiot!"

Robert could not help laughing. Even in the midst of tragedy, there would certainly be some comedic relief if Spigot were around.

He became serious again. "I can't understand how it is possible that Cristina agreed to become engaged to that worm! The circumstances, you must admit, are at least a bit suspicious. Only the last time I saw her, when we rescued her from your friend, The Polack," and he motioned to Spigot, "I told her we needed to talk, she and I. I am sure she understood the meaning of my words. Now, see here," he reasoned and started counting on his fingers: "The day after, without any explanation, she simply quits her job at the music store. Then she was gone somewhere to take care of a sick relative—whose name or relationship to her were never explained. Then this guy, Daniel, constantly visiting the house at all hours. Finally, out of the blue, they are engaged. Too mysterious if you ask me."

"Maybe you are not so irresistible as you think you are, *mon vieux*," was Spigot's dismissive comment, which received a venomous look from Max.

Robert shook his head. "If you saw her face when I first entered that house a few minutes ago, you'd not think that, Frog."

They finally drained the rest of the whiskey, paid, and left.

\* \* \*

A couple of hours after Robert and his cronies had left

Cristina's house, Eugênio rang the doorbell. He had gone to shore to buy some needed goods, ignorant of the latest events that had taken place, and took the opportunity to see how things were with his girlfriend. He was inspecting the damaged to the door when it was opened by Maria. The troubled look on her face was somewhat abated as she saw who the caller was.

"Oh, Eugênio!"

"Is everything all right?" he asked, surprised at her expression, and significantly glancing at the damaged door.

She followed his gazed: "Oh, that. It was your boss," was the disconcerting answer.

"My boss? What do you mean?" He shot an amazed look at her.

"We cannot talk here. Let's go for a walk. Wait here while I get rid of this apron and fetch my hat."

She was back presently and, crossing the street, they reached the sidewalk on the shore side. They strolled in silence for several minutes, observing the black and white undulating design under their feet. Then she started to speak, rather to unburden herself to him. Eugênio listened in silence and the more he did, the more clouded his countenance became.

"This is serious business. You understand that I must tell this to Mr. Laughton."

"Of course! You must go straight to him and tell it all. Maybe he can find a way to break this outrageous engagement."

"Oh, I am sure he will find a way, don't you worry." And taking Maria back to the house, he startled her by giving her a kiss. He then left with the promise that something would be done, that she should stop worrying.

* * *

Eugênio found Robert in his room with his two cronies plus the ubiquitous Bunky, all of whom were given permission to stay. As he finished his recitation, Robert was dumbfounded, and the other three listeners manifested their outrage in high volume and profusion.

"What I would very much like to know is how that sewer rat got hold of this promissory note—especially since there was never any effort to collect," Robert commented when he was finally able to express himself. "And I wonder who this mysterious creditor might be." But in the back of his mind a suspicion took hold of him. The idea was monstrous, but considering the man he suspected, it all seemed to fit and elucidate the mystery.

"Should we pay a little visit to the sewer rat and put the screws to him?" asked Bunky, clenching his large fists, his normally cold blue eyes shining with excitement.

"Remember that you no longer are a street thug," Robert wagged a finger at him. Then appearing amenable: "But I cannot dismiss the possibilities your suggestion raises. I think you have a point there, Bunky." Turning to Eugênio: "Do you have the sewer rat's address, Eugênio?"

"Yes, sir. Miss Maria wrote it down on a piece of paper for me," and he handed it to Robert.

"Thank you, Eugênio. I think you might have helped us save Miss Cristina from this imbroglio."

"Can I be of any more help, sir?"

"No, you have done more than I could have ever hoped for—or repay."

And the young man left with a contented expression. He directed his steps to the kitchen where he found his canine companion eagerly awaiting him.

As Max and Spigot started making strategic plans, Desiree entered the room and the dialogue was interrupted.

"Why did you stop talking?" she enquired of the silent group.

"The subject was not suitable for ladies," was Robert's quick answer.

"As if you ever cared how you express yourself when I am around," was his relative's ungracious, if nevertheless truthful, comment. "But I know when I am not wanted," and she turned her nose up and left.

"Perhaps you better go with her, Max. Make sure she won't be in our way. I'll have a quick lunch—I haven't eaten for hours— and Bunky will go around to tell you when I am ready. Maybe you two should also at something."

"*Oui, mon capitain.*" The Fenchman said and gave a mock salute before he left.

155

"I thought they were never going to leave. Quickly, Bunky, help me here so we can skip boat before those two realize they've been had. This is not a job to be accomplished by a crowd. And who knows, there may be some unsavory story I'd rather not share with anyone else."

"So, we're going to put the screws to the punk after all. Swell," said a grinning Bunky while he helped Robert's good arm into his jacket. "Although on an empty stomach..."

"Well, perhaps I should spare you the horrors of an empty stomach and leave you here to enjoy your meal," said Robert, and faced the mirror to give his hair a quick brush.

As he turned to get his hat, Bunky hurried to his room to get his garments and met him on the deserted deck. They jumped into the launch and, as Bunky maneuvered it, Robert turned back to see his two frustrated friends waving helplessly from the yacht. He waved back, getting clenched fists in response to his impudence. He instructed Bunky to direct the launch to the little pier of the Flamengo neighborhood. This pier served the Palácio do Catete (the seat of the President) and the Flamengo Regatta Club.

On shore, after a fifteen minute walk through the Beira Mar Avenue, they veered right and, skirting the imposing building of the Hotel Central that stood in that corner, turned into the street. Robert read the street name: "Barão do Flamengo." Then he and Bunky found the house they were looking for and examined it briefly. It was a portly old house, not unlike all the others on the street. The place was silent, almost all the shutters closed.

"Shall we give the front door your treatment, Master Robert?" Bunky asked, a nasty gleam in his eye.

Robert ignored the joke and rang the bell. After a long wait, the door opened just enough to let them see Daniel's face. He gave a sharp air intake and slammed the door shut.

"Like a deer in the headlights," growled Bunky. "Seems the gent doesn't have fond memories of you. Wonder why."

Ignoring the repartee, Robert yelled: "Do you want me to break the door?" The question might not have been grammatically correct in Portuguese but had its intended effect and presently the door opened.

"What do you want?" Daniel asked while backing away a

few steps to a safe distance.

"I want to talk," answered Robert as he entered the house followed by Bunky.

"And shove your face in the toilet bowl again, punk," put in Bunky. "I hope you're thirsty!"

"He doesn't understand English, you nitwit," was Robert's irritated comment in English, then turning to Daniel he continued in Portuguese: "I know you forced Miss Cristina into this engagement through blackmail."

"You have no right to come to my house to insult me! My engagement is none of your business!"

"Come again?" Bunky inquired of Robert.

"Shut up, Bunky, or I'll put *your* head in the toilet bowl!"

"Oh, that would be the day," and Bunky gave a loud, hearty laugh.

"Be quiet while I try to get information. You're not helping." Then turning again to Daniel, he explained in halting Portuguese: "Listen, I know how you forced Cristina. I know about the promissory. I want to know the address of the person who holds it."

"I won't tell you! You can't force me," Daniel answered, his voice in a crescendo, trying to give it an assurance he was far from feeling.

"I do not want to hurt you, but I will if you don't answer."

Daniel crossed his arms in front of his chest and shook his head again. Although Bunky did not understand a word of the dialogue, he understood that. Swiftly he covered the few steps that separated him from Daniel and, before Robert knew what was happening, grabbed the little man by his collar, raised him from the floor and held him at arm's length. Daniel feebly paddled his feet in the air as Bunky shook him like a rag doll: "Listen here, sewer rat, spill it or I'll give you another hair wash," he roared.

"OK, Bunky, he's getting purple. Let him go, he got the message," was Robert's calm request.

Bunky obeyed and Daniel fell to the floor with a grunt.

"Attaboy, Bunky!" Robert patted him on the back. "Let's see if you didn't damage his vocal cords." And turning to Daniel: "Now, tell me—"

Robert did not need to finish his demand. Daniel was

already talking in a choked, gasping voice, one hand gingerly massaging his neck: "It was Mr. Rebelo de Oliveira, who had the promissory note! It was *his* idea!"

This merely confirmed Robert's suspicion of who the holder of the promissory was, so he cut to the chase: "I want his address," he said sternly, and when Daniel started to refuse, Robert merely looked at Bunky. As the huge man advanced on him, Daniel squealed and expelled a torrent of information.

Before leaving Robert told Daniel in so many words that if he ever heard of him approaching Cristina, he would kill him— words which, although spoken in Portuguese, Bunky felt sure of the meaning and controlled himself not to pat his boy on the back.

With the address of Alexandre Rebelo de Oliveira, they jumped into the first taxi cab they found when they reached the Beira Mar Avenue. Robert instructed the driver to go to the railroad station at Formosa beach. As an incentive, he told the man, he would double the fare if he were able to get them to the station in fifteen minutes.

"And all this because of a skirt," mumbled Bunky.

"Bunky," Robert growled in a low voice. "I am not in the mood for your silliness."

At the railway station, they got the first train to Petrópolis. The trip was made mostly in silence, Robert being upset with the turn of events. Bunky, having nothing to contribute, sat back and, lulled by the motion of the train, his loud snores filled the air.

A little over two hours later they arrived at the Petrópolis station where they caught a cab and were soon standing in front of one of the town's stately mansions.

"Bunky, behave," said Robert, as he rang the bell. And looking at the big man with twinkling eyes, he continued: "I don't think we have to rough anyone up. But just in case, you go in first." At which comment Bunky gave a little snort.

The same sepulchral looking majordomo who, several days before, had introduced Daniel into the house, opened the door.

"*Oy veh*," Bunky whispered, as he cocked a stunned eye at the man.

"I would like to see Mr. Alexandre Rebelo de Oliveira," said Robert and handed the man his card.

The haughty majordomo opened the door wide and asked

Robert to step in, sparing a dubious glance at Bunky. And as the latter started to make his way in, Robert turned to him with a restraining gesture: "Wait outside." And the door was unceremoniously closed on the large man's fuming face.

Left to cool his heels in front of the house, Bunky's thoughts verged on murder. He enjoyed imagining many versions of a repeating scene: a very young Robert rushing into a street packed with cars while he, Bunky, now held back the hand that had once reached out to save the boy. And they say one should learn from one's mistakes, he thought, and shook his head, disgruntled.

Inside the house Robert was shown to the same room in which Daniel had once waited for the man who, he was convinced, could grant his most cherished wish. He did not have to wait long before the two men found themselves standing face to face. Alexandre's cold eyes peered into Robert's. He saw in them calm but also resolve. He had received a call from a highly agitated Daniel and was expecting the young man's visit. Daniel—what a hindrance that young man had become, he thought, while he observed the American. Daniel had become an uncomfortable link with a past he thought buried; and where that man was concerned, he decided he needed to take steps to make sure it remained buried. His somber thoughts were interrupted by Robert.

"I am sure you know why I am here," said Robert in English, after they had briefly exchanged greetings and his host had showed him to a chair. "Name your price for the promissory note."

Alexandre's eyebrows shot up slightly. The shadow of a smirk twisted his lips and Robert had an overwhelming urge to punch them, which was duly repressed but did not escape Alexandre's watchful gaze. "I am impressed with your devotion to the young lady, Mr. Laughton," he answered in impeccable English. "Few would propose to spend so lavishly on behalf of one woman. Your dedication is touching."

"I am not interested in your opinion. Let's do business and I'll be on my way." With a herculean effort he kept emotion from his voice, his face reflecting his control.

"Very well," Alexandre agreed, his long fingers meeting at the tips while he rested his elbows on the chair arms.

"How much?" The question had been uttered with intended

slowness.

The sum mentioned meant Robert would be almost completely clean of capital after it was met; yet, without batting an eyelid, he requested and was granted the use of the Louis XV writing table. What might he have felt had he known this table held the document he agreed to buy? Extracting his check book from his jacket's inside pocket, he sat down to write the check.

"You will understand the need to leave the bearer's name out." The silky tone in Alexandre's voice jarred on Robert's high strung nerves.

He carefully tore the page off, controlling himself not to damage it, and, going to Alexandre's chair, offered the check to him, withholding it as the other made to take it: "First, I want to see the document."

"Fair enough." Alexandre went to the desk Robert had just left, unlocked a drawer, and removed a folded piece of paper. He turned to the young man and, extending his hand that held the paper, asked, "Shall we exchange them simultaneously?"

As he took possession of the paper and released the check, Robert intently read through it and, raising his eyes, addressed Alexandre: "I assume this is the original and there are no copies or outstanding debts," he said and which the other confirmed with a nod.

Robert went to the fireplace, lit a match, and touched it to the paper. He kept it until, almost completely consumed, the flame touched his finger when he let the charred, unrecognizable little bits fall into the hearth. He then turned to his opponent, who watched him with a cold expression. "As honor is a concept you clearly do not understand," Robert started and had the pleasure of seeing the other blanch, "I won't waste my time asking you to give your word of honor that you will leave the young lady in question alone—as well as anyone related to her. I will merely stress that I would do anything to spare her the knowledge of this sordid business. *Anything*," he stressed, and, without taking his eyes from Alexandre, pulled aside his jacket just enough to expose a holster. He turned on his heels and went out of the room, leaving the other man speechless.

Alexandre went to the window in time to see Robert and Bunky leaving. Well, isn't this young man brave, he thought. He comes accompanied by a veritable Hercules, but leaves him outside and enters the enemy's den by himself. Remarkable! Then his eyes fell on the piece of paper he had been holding. He turned to the fireplace and, lighting a match, let it consume the check. This done he went to the desk and pressed a gilded leaf on its side. A little panel sprang open, exposing a small compartment. From it he extracted the photograph of a young woman in a long, white dress with a lace train, her narrow waist held by a wide velvet sash. She stood very straight in half profile. Large eyes peered from a face of classic beauty. A wide-brimmed hat from whence three dark feathers sprang sat at an angle over the lustrous waves of her black hair, pulled up loosely. Her long neck was encased in a web of delicate lace—the same that covered the yoke and the sleeves. In her ungloved hands she held a small bouquet. On the wrist of her left arm, a bracelet incrusted with highly polished black onyx gleamed softly. It matched necklace, earrings, and ring.

His eyes on the picture, he slowly returned to the fireplace. He again took a match and, instead of touching it to the striker on the side of the container, after briefly hesitating, returned it to the others. He smiled sadly at the photograph, walked back to the desk, and returned it to its concealing place. "You see, I cannot strike you out of my life completely, countess." He did not realize he had uttered the words out loud.

He went to the door and called his henchmen, then sat down in one of the chairs facing the extinct fireplace. When the two young men had entered, they respectfully waited to be addressed.

"I have two tasks for those two men that you last hired. They are to go to the docs and find a cargo ship soon returning to some faraway place—I don't care where, so long as it is a long trip. They will give the captain this envelope," and he proceeded to fill it with money. "The captain will take on a passenger; he must keep the passenger isolated from the crew at all times. The money will be an incentive, I am sure." He handed the envelope to the brothers and continued: "Then the men will go to a house at Barão do Flamengo Street and discreetly—mind my words: discreetly—get Mr. Daniel Cabral to accompany them to the docs, where he will be handed over to the captain."

Castor, the more communicative of the two brothers, asked,

"Would you not prefer that we perform this task, sir? It sounds a bit delicate—"

"Absolutely not," Alexandre cut him off. "I want no involvement in this, in case it misfires. As these two men don't know your real names, they cannot connect you with me. This must be done in total secrecy. Understood?" Receiving their acknowledgment, he continued: "They will find a certain private detective, a Ramirez—they must look up his address, but it is downtown, so it will not be too difficult to find. He seems to frequent an establishment called Bar Adolph, if I recall Mr. Cabral's story. At any rate, this detective must be dealt with in a more definite manner." No further explanation was necessary, for the twins clearly understood the meaning. "He talks too much when in his cups, so no trip to a faraway place will work in this case, unfortunately for him."

"It will be done, sir. You can rest assured," was Castor's answer. The twins left and Alexandre remained, with the ghosts of his past.

* * *

If Daniel had consulted the gypsy he'd encountered that very day just before getting home, she might have told him the future held for him not marriage but a long sea voyage. That it would not be of his choice, the gypsy might not disclose to him. As for Ramirez, the police closed the case on him after his drowned body was found by fishermen. He had been a trader in illegal drugs and had done very little detecting—that side of his business being generally used to blackmail the clients who actually became his victims. He would not be missed, and as for his girlfriend, Dulce, she was not unhappy to see him vanish from her life, as well as the purple eye he had left her as a souvenir.

# CHAPTER 10

In the train, on their way back to Rio, Bunky disgorged his outrage at the treatment he'd received when trying to enter Alexandre's house.

"Did you have to let that lackey slam the door at my face?"

The man's injured expression was comical. "Bunky, I do apologize, but I wanted to use my secret weapon only as a last resort." And as this did not elicit a single comment, the rest of the trip was made in silence, Bunky having obstinately kept his face turned to the window.

When they stepped out of the train in Rio, the sun had gone down but the heat had not abated. The humidity was almost suffocating, especially after the cool, dry air they had enjoyed in Petrópolis—but this fact did not help allay Bunky's bruised pride. Noticing that his pal's injured silence persisted, Robert tried to make amends.

"Bunky, I know I have been difficult these last days," at which comment the other snorted, but Robert continued: "but I am under a certain amount of pressure. It is not only my feelings that are involved in this case. There is a lot you don't know." And here he saw clear signs he had stirred Bunky's curiosity—the man's Achilles heel. "Let's walk to the harbor and I'll tell you the whole thing."

* * *

Early the next morning the ship *S.S. American Legion* of the Pan America Line arrived, carrying John Laughton and the "countess." Robert was there with Bunky, who had insisted he should go to shore with him and act as a bodyguard if necessary. The rest of the party had remained on the yacht after Robert insisted that he had private matters to discuss with both travelers.

After a long interval, when the two passengers had gone through customs, they finally met Robert. Their greetings accomplished, Robert's shoulder was duly noticed, decried, and explained, and Bunky was teased for not being at hand to help Master Robert. The travelers were then taken to the luxurious Avenida Hotel, downtown, not far from the harbor—Robert thought the Copacabana Palace would not be the best place to stash the "countess" for the time being, at least until she decided how she wanted to proceed.

Arriving at the hotel, Robert begged the lady some time alone with his father and they met in the latter's room. "I know you are tired, father."

"Not at all, I am hankering for the company of men. I spent eleven days cooped up in that huge bathtub. Besides, as gracious as our countess is, I tell you, I had enough at being a lady's maid; at $450 round trip each, it is no joke, I tell you," at which words Robert grinned. "Yes, go ahead and laugh. But believe me when I tell you it's no laughing matter, my boy. We could not squeeze her maid in, so I had to assume some of her duties. Every evening I was called to her room and asked how she looked, if I thought she should change anything in her outfit, if the blue looked better than the gray outfit. I know nothing of these matters and tried to sound nice and just told her she looked marvelous in whatever she chose. After the second time, I found myself in trouble, accused of being a liar, of not caring for the way she presented herself at dinner, and who knows what else because she reverted to Russian. I can't tell you the tough time I had, and I am too happy it is over," he said and finished his grouse with a long "phew." "I just hope I don't have to resume my duties on the way back, Robert. Perhaps I will sneak onto the yacht if you can find some corner for me."

His son laughed at his genitor's idea and told him he was welcome on his own yacht any time, but he then turned serious. "Now, father, I must tell you of some developments. I think the countess should be told it all, but I will let you decided."

John Laughton listened attentively, without interrupting his son. Afterwards he suggested that they should call on the countess so Robert could repeat to her what he had told him.

"There is one thing I do not believe the countess should know," he told his father. "I think you will agree that it would hurt her tremendously—and, to that extent, her daughter. I would rather we do not disclose my meeting with Alexandre Rebelo de Oliveira. It would be better if she continued to believe him dead," and at the thought of that meeting, he tightened his fists and his knuckles grew white.

His father having agreed with him, they had a long conversation with the lady Robert called "countess." While the young man spoke, she realized his interest in her situation had been increased by his unmistakable infatuation for Cristina. It was decided that Robert would take her to Cristina's house in the morning while his father stayed on the yacht. Robert would give instructions to the crew that the yacht should be moored at the Copacabana beach.

As had been agreed, Robert waited in the lobby of the Avenida Hotel the next morning. At that same time, Cristina was leaving her house. Her head covered with a delicate mantilla of white lace, she walked the quiet Atlântica Avenue, her troubled eyes not seeing the majestic panorama to her left—the sun-kissed, limpid, aqua-marine ocean that reflected the cloudless sky above it. The air was still cool, but, deep in thought, she did not pay attention to these external details. She veered right onto Hilário de Gouvêia Street and had not far to walk until she reached the door of Nossa Senhora de Copacabana church—Our Lady of Copacabana.

The first Mass had already ended. She entered that holy place, and the quiet, as it always did when she was troubled, worked its magic: she felt calmer than she had in the last few days. She reached for the holy water, made the sign of the cross, and walked through the aisles of pews to kneel in the last bench, facing the altar. There, half an hour later, the vicar found her in the same position, the rosary between fervently clasped fingers. Seeing the young woman so absorbed in prayer, he decided not to disturb her and left her to her meditations. The last muffled echoes of his steps reverberated through the empty church when Cristina rose and, making the sign of the cross, walked down the aisle toward the large entrance door.

She had prayed for guidance and had meditated on the latest events that had befallen her life, and she felt, even if not completely sure of what steps to take, at least somewhat appeased. As she came out of the building, the inescapable beauty of the morning overcame her. She smiled despite her troubles. When she came upon Atlântica Avenue, she crossed it and stood at the mosaic sidewalk watching the azure of the horizon mate with the sea. The picture that met her eyes was enchanting: a ribbon of cream-colored sand where small waves broke at short intervals reflecting a myriad of colors, while beyond the sea was a mass of deep blue. She peered around and, seeing no one, stepped from the sidewalk onto the soft sand and discretely removed her shoes, lowered her garters, and removed the stockings. The wet sand massaged her feet that the crystalline waves caressed, covering the imprints they left. How many times had her footprints been left in these sands to be obliterated by the waves? She watched as small shells that mingled with the sand were thrown about by the revolving water. They so perfectly reflected her life; her lips actually curved in the shadow of a smile—a somewhat bitter one. Like those waves, life circumstances impelled her, like the helpless shells. And her mind recollected the last events that had befallen her. Faces, fragments of conversations, scenes, like disjointed clips from a movie, projected on her mind's screen. But above all Robert's face kept recurring, with its alluring smile and frank stare. After several minutes of walking, she decided it was time to return home. It was time to face the troubles she knew awaited her—for no matter how much she prayed, how much she delayed facing them, there was no escaping and she must inevitably address them.

* * *

The bell rang and Maria ran to the front door. Cristina had probably forgotten her veil or her rosary—yet in the back of her mind was the incipient memory that the girl had a key. The smile died on her lips and gave way to startled surprise: Robert stood there. With him was a very pretty lady. It was but a moment of hesitation before the young man spoke, but Maria had the odd impression that there was something familiar about the lady.

"Good morning, Maria," Robert's voice broke the awkward silence. "I know it is terribly early, but can we come in?"

Embarrassed, she stepped aside and, her eyes fastened on the lady, realized where she had seen that face. It was like, she thought, Cristina would look when older. She saw the lady smile at her and the similarity became even more remarkable.

"Is Mrs. Abramov in?"

Maria almost jumped at Robert's question, so intently had she been watching his companion, and felt ashamed at her behavior. "Yes," she was able to respond in a not very steady voice.

"And do you think we might be allowed to speak with her?" he patiently asked Maria, whose confusion he noticed.

"I will let her know that you and," she hesitated, "a lady are here to see her. Please, would you wait in the living room?" She led them there and left, assuring she would be back directly with some *cafezinho*.

Robert explained to his puzzled companion—who seemed to somehow follow the exchange—that *cafezinho* was a ubiquitous tiny cup of coffee, a symbol of Brazilian hospitality, no matter the time of day, which delighted her; not so long ago she had broken her fast with that same beverage, yet it would again be offered her as refreshment.

Robert could not help being amazed at her calm, considering the gravity of her errand. But, again, the lady was always able to remain collected at stressful moments, which, he reflected, diverged from her offspring's somewhat fiery reactions.

A few minutes later Maria was back with a tray on which sat two tiny cups filled with steamy coffee, a sugar bowl, and two immaculately white starched napkins. "Mrs. Abramov will be here presently," she responded shyly to the lady's beautiful face. For a second she almost bowed—for she thought she had guessed who Robert's companion was—but, resisting the urge, left the room.

Not long afterwards a woman appeared in the doorway: it was Mrs. Abramov. Robert's companion shot up from her seat, as if impelled by an invisible spring, and he followed suit. He heard Mrs. Abramov's strangled voice but was not sure what she said. Her hand stole to her chest and her face blanched. As she stepped into the room, her legs faltered. She reeled and Robert caught hold of her before she could fall. He helped her to the sofa and his companion loosed the neck of her dress while gently speaking to her in a foreign language that Robert concluded was Russian.

He looked at the woman on the sofa in utter amazement. He had not yet met Sonya Abramov, yet he would have never conceived the mother of that lovely, dark creature could be this stocky woman of middle age. Strands of blond hair mingled with a grizzled mass of gray, and the whole was caught into a large bun at the nape of a wide neck. The face was not unbecoming but marred by a low forehead. The close-set, greyish eyes would have imparted a furtive mien, were it not for the wrinkles at their corners that spoke of a merry soul; she had high cheekbones and a wide mouth, sided by two deep creases. Bemused, he observed the recumbent figure and wondered how Cristina could have been so deceived. Not even the slightest likeness could be found between her and this woman.

Robert heard his companion's soft voice address him in very heavily accented English: "Perhaps you could wait in another room, my dear." She turned to Mrs. Abramov, who was giving signs of recovering, then back to Robert: "I believe we will be better if left by ourselves. You understand, don't you?" she asked, laying on his cuff a delicate hand on which a large onyx ring sparkled.

"I was going to suggest something of the sort," he said and patted her hand. "You noticed the big building when we drove by, not far from here? It is a hotel, with a terrace on the front, and I will wait there. It is easy to see this house from there, so I will be able to notice if you come out." And before she could object, he said, "It is better if I am out of the way. This is a very private conversation. I will be all right," he reassured her. "I know I will find an American newspaper in the hotel."

In the meantime Mrs. Abramov had recovered and tried to get up but was held down by the lady's firm hand on her shoulder. Before Robert left the room, he saw Mrs. Abramov, tears in her eyes, grasp the other's hand and kiss it while mumbling words in a foreign language.

* * *

Cristina discreetly cleaned the sand from her feet, put on her shoes, and rolled stockings and garters into a ball. As she reached the sidewalk and started to cross the street to get to her house, her eyes twinkled with a mischievous light at the thought of how shocked her mother and Maria would be if they knew she was out in the street barelegged. And had she done it forty minutes earlier, she would have been surprised at the sight of Robert walking out of her house's gate and, turning to his left, purposely heading in the direction of the Copacabana Palace. Not having seen him, she entered through the gate without a second thought.

While she put on her stockings in the entrance hall, she heard her mother and another feminine voice conversing, she believed, in Russian. Following the direction of the sounds, she came to the living room and halted at the threshold. Her mother abruptly stopped speaking. Cristina turned to the other occupant of the room, unknown to her. That lady— her posture was clearly that of a lady—stood up and was followed by Mrs. Abramov.

The lady's large, black eyes that sparkled like black diamonds were intent on the girl's. She was about Cristina's height and slim. Her elegant dress was a pale yellow, printed georgette with a one-sided jabot, tied at the hips, and had a godet flounce. The high-heeled shoes mimicked the yellow of the dress. Her black hair, which showed just a few streaks of grey, complemented the ivory of her skin. It was worked in perfectly symmetrical finger waves, collected in a bun on the nape of her neck. The effect of the whole was very sophisticated, yet discreet. But what really caught Cristina's eye was the beautiful face. It had something familiar; what, she could not quite define. Had she happened to look at a mirror, she would have been surprised at what it would have revealed.

In a soft, melodious voice, the lady said something in Russian that, Cristina thought, meant "my dear Tinoshka"; that puzzled her because it was her parents' pet name for her. Extending both hands she smiled in such a sweet, inviting way that the girl surrendered hers to the tender grasp. Cristina saw the beautiful eyes fill with tears. She looked at her mother, enquiringly.

"This is the Countess Helena Alexandrovna Dobrinsky, Cristina," she answered the girl's unuttered question.

At this the countess softly admonished Mrs. Abramov in Russian: "Now, Sonyushka, no more of that." And turning to Cristina, said in perfect French: "I was a countess a long, long time ago. My name is simply Helena McCarthy. Now, why don't we sit down?" And she gave Cristina's hands a light squeeze before directing the girl to the sofa, where she sat between the two women. "I have a story to tell you."

"I will leave the two of you alone."

"No, Sonyushka, do not go, please," was the answer in Russian.

An ex-Countess, Cristina pondered, even more mystified. Her mother had never said anything about being acquainted with a countess.

"I do not know how to start," she hesitated, then seemed to decide. "Perhaps I should just start at the beginning. There, we already made a little bit of progress, haven't we?" she looked kindly at Cristina and took the girl's hands into hers; they were soft and warm, and it was done in such unaffected way Cristina thought it was just natural that this unknown woman would hold her hands. "When I was very young—I was not yet twenty, mind you—I became a widow. I was not pained by the loss, as mine was not a happy marriage. You see, it was arranged and he was much older. Shortly after becoming a widow, I lost a child; it was born dead." Her voice betrayed emotion that was quickly controlled. "That devastated me so much that my mother thought a change of scenery would do me good. But also because she knew I had fallen madly in love and wanted to separate me from this man." She looked straight into Cristina's eyes: "From your father."

Cristina took in a sharp breath and tried to pull her hands from the other's grasp, but she was not let go. She turned shocked eyes to Sonya, who, having been raised with Helena, understood French and had followed the conversation. "It is all right," she told the girl. "Listen to the end and you will understand."

"As I told you," the countess continued, "being married very young to a man so much older, I was very unhappy but tried to accept my lot in life. However, you see, destiny played a trick on me: it sent this fascinating young man into my life. My husband and I were in Moscow and attended all kinds of parties. He did not dance, but at that time couples were not very particular about being constantly together, so while I was never allowed to sit while the orchestra played, nothing seemed amiss." Her eyes suddenly acquired a dreamy look, reflecting the magic of that past she now recounted. "He was a fascinating young man, so tall and proud, so handsome, so elegant," she continued to Cristina. "It all seemed so natural that we fell in love—young and so infatuated with each other, the whole world seemed to be conspiring to unite us. But then my husband had a stroke and was confined to bed. By that time my mother—who was a domineering woman and still ruled me with an iron fist—had realized my involvement and convinced my husband he should return to his estate, where, not long after, he died. A few of months later I lost my child. I was devastated and, you see, my mother took me to this little town in Portugal where I remained for a year, languishing despite the salutary sea air that was supposed to restore me to health," she said.

"I will never know how he found me again—as all forms of communication were not only difficult at that time but forbidden to me. Nevertheless, we met and we escaped in the middle of the night to Paris. Imagine my joy: I was in one of the most romantic cities in the world—where I had spent a few years in a finishing school—with the man I loved." And her expression betrayed how much the past still lived inside her. "He was from Brazil and his family called him back. They had decided it was time he married and had chosen a young lady from an aristocratic family. We agreed he should go to Brazil and tell his family he was going to marry me, instead. He needed time to convince them, but he was sure he would succeed. He then would arrange for my visit. We were to be married there." The pleasure of that memory was evident in her face.

"I embarked on a study of all things Brazilian, found a teacher and started dreaming. When I escaped Portugal, I took with me two faithful servants—friends, actually. We had grown up together. They were children of the house servants, but despite our class difference—Russians had a very marked cast system, you know—my mother actually allowed them to be my childhood companions. They came to work for me, as a couple, when I married. So while my beloved was in Brazil, my two friends joined me in my Portuguese classes. And, oh, did we have fun," she laughed. "It was then that I realized I was, well, in an interesting condition. You understand?" To this Cristina assented.

The countess continued her story: "Time passed and no news came from Brazil and I became frantic. My child was born—that precious, precious blessing from God—but my anxiety grew, for no news came my way. I decided to go to the Brazilian embassy. He worked for the diplomatic corps, but I had refrained from contacting the embassy for fear of causing some kind of trouble for him. They gave me the news that he had died in a car accident." Here Cristina gasped and tighten her hold on the lady's hand. "He had been travelling to meet his family in their town—Petrópolis it was. I was devastated. I somehow dragged myself back to the house I was living in, and my dear friends, the couple I just told you of, tried everything they could to raise me from the catatonic-like state I fell into. Desperate, they got hold of my mother, and she arrived like the winter Mistral, blowing aside everything in her way!

"She found a doctor in Paris to treat me. When I was able to understand, she told me she had thought much while I was half-conscious and had concluded the child had to be accepted by the father's family. She had also gotten busy and had a marriage certificate—counterfeit, of course—that would be presented to the family. When I protested, for it was a terrible lie, she convinced me I should think of my child. She would be sent ahead, and when I was sufficiently recovered, she, my mother, would return to travel with me to Brazil. My mother obtained his family's address and wrote a letter explaining everything. She sent the family instructions about my little darling's arrival and that we would follow once I was strong. So they went, my two friends, carrying the counterfeit document and my very life: my child. In the days that followed, I realized the terrible mistake I had made, and I had a relapse. But I was young and soon was well again. I was still quite weak and my mother did not have much difficulty convincing me that everything would end well. One beautiful sunny day, I insisted she should go out, for she had been cooped up with me all this time. She decided on a boat trip on the river Seine. My mother was never a spendthrift in the best of times; with my illness and all the expenses with the house and the trip, she decided to hire an inexpensive skiff for a short trip with a lady friend. The thing floundered and my mother and her friend drowned."

She took a deep breath. Seeing Cristina's sad expression she patted the girl's hand and continued. "As my mother did not return, the doctor treating me, Dr. Bellerose, took a kind interest in my situation and inquired in hospitals and finally went to the city morgue where he identified her. She had been carrying her address book with her, but it was lost in the drowning. With her gone I now had only my child left. That same day I got a letter from Brazil: the response to my mother's. Reading it was almost the death of me. It denied their son having ever mentioned me and implied ours was an attempt to besmirch his memory by imputing an out-of-wedlock child upon him. It nevertheless confirmed his death.

"I am not going to go into the details of that terrible time," she said and looked sadly at Cristina. "By losing contact with my friends, who were sent to Brazil with my child, I lost her, too, so you can imagine how I suffered. It was Gary—the man I soon afterwards married—who saved my life. He never knew the truth but thought I had lost both husband and child. As I never wanted him to know my past, I never undeceived him. He died a few years ago—the most wonderful man; I wish so much you could have met him, my dear—and I decided to try to find out the fate of my lost child. John Laughton—Robert's father—helped me." She saw the girl's puzzled expression. "Laughton was a great friend of my Gary. Through his contacts he hired a discreet investigator in Rio, where I at least knew my friends would have disembarked all those years ago. And this is the reason why I am here: to find my daughter." She took a deep breath and, after a few seconds of hesitation, added: "To find you, my beloved daughter."

* * *

The words were delivered in such a calm, matter-of-fact tone that it fairly took Cristina's breath away. She was too astonished to make any comment and stood for a while gazing at the woman's beautiful face. She thought she had not understood her words. But, no, she had heard correctly, for she spoke and understood French perfectly. There was no mistake: she had called Cristina "*ma chère fille*," my beloved daughter. But there *must* be some mistake, Cristina thought. She turned to Sonya Abramov, but even without a word being exchanged, the other woman's eyes carried the confirmation of that remarkable story.

Slowly she stood up and took a few steps away from the sofa, her fingers absently toying with the onyx bracelet on her wrist. The two women remained seated, watching her intently. The room was very quiet, like a world apart from everything else. Cristina had the impression that if she turned back to the sofa it would be empty. But she knew it would not be so and that certainty made her hesitate. Somehow, that sad, pungent story must be true, otherwise it would have been denied by her mother—oh, how could she come to call her Sonya, and not mother? And then it occurred to her that that very morning, she had prayed for a miracle. And wasn't this the most extraordinary one that just happened? She turned and faced the two anxious, silent women. It was then that she saw the onyx ring on the countess's finger. It perfectly matched her bracelet. Her thoughts were truly chaotic, yet there was a sense of betrayal that predominated above her general bewilderment. Down inside she revolted against having been lied to her whole life!

"I wrapped it around your tiny little wrist before you left," the lady said, and looked at Cristina's wrist. The beautiful eyes welled up with tears that started to slowly run down the woman's face. "My darling, I can't believe I found you." And standing up she walked to

172

Cristina and wrapped the girl in a tight embrace.

It took Cristina a few seconds to realize she had remained limp while being embraced. And with the realization, it came to her that everything that happened, the sad story she had been told, was no one's fault. Nobody conspired to lie to her; they did so to protect her from suffering. The Abramovs never meant her harm; they did what they thought was best in such strained circumstances. They actually protected her and treated her as if she were their true child. And her mother—she would have to get used to calling her that—her mother had been left alone and helpless. She asked herself what she might have done if left in the same situation.

Her arms slowly returned the embrace, and her mother's body shook with uncontrollable sobs. Minutes later she disengaged her arms from Cristina and held the girl at arms' length, analyzing her face. "I do not know if I will ever look at you enough, my darling," she said, smiling through her tears. Then something occurred to her and her countenance became serious: "I wonder if you will ever forgive me taking so long to find you?"

The girl took her hand, and pressed it in both hers: "Of course...mother," she exclaimed. And the word sounded just right; there was no awkwardness anymore.

Helena was unable to answer, for tears of joy and gratitude were again running down her cheeks. "How pathetic must I look," she whispered, and turning to Sonya, noticed the other's red-rimmed eyes. "We both look, Sonyushka," she said, and keeping Cristina's hand in hers, went back to the sofa, where she kissed her friend's cheek. "I will never be able to thank you for keeping and caring for my precious child. You *are* her mother, if not by blood, at least by rights."

"We tried to get in touch with you, but you had already left France, and we had no idea where you'd gone," Sonya lamented.

"I know, my dear. You and Vasili did what was right and I will always be in your debt." She extracted a dainty cambric handkerchief from her purse and, dabbing her eyes, turned to Cristina and resumed speaking French: "I know we have so much to talk about, my darling, but there is someone who I know is anxious to see you. Would you come with me on a short walk?"

Mother and daughter left the house and, arm in arm, strolled on the sidewalk, on the shore side. The blue sea shone like a gigantic sapphire.

"Vasili's debt has been taken care of, so this engagement can be broken. That is, if you do not care for this gentleman, Daniel," her mother was saying. And at the girl's surprise added, "I was informed of everything concerning you, my dear."

"He is no gentleman, mother." The word sent a warm waive through her heart every time she uttered it: *mother*. She now had two mothers, Cristina thought, thrilled.

"Well, then you can follow your heart. If you love someone else, my darling," she allowed the sentence to hang in the air, and in her eyes a mischievous light shone.

Before the girl could say anything, she saw Robert stride out of the Copacabana Palace, cross the street and move purposefully in their direction.

"I think there is something that young man might like to ask you, my dear. Go to him." She smiled at Cristina and gently disengaged her arm after kissing her brow. She stood watching while her daughter went to meet Robert Laughton. The young man had helped her retrieve her lost treasure, which she was about to lose again. Well, not exactly lose, she corrected herself. Marriage would not stop her from seeing her Cristina. She retraced her steps to the Abramov's house where she knew her best friend, Sonya, awaited her and would be glad at the news she would bring her.

As they approached each other, Cristina and Robert felt they were alone in the world. They did not notice the yacht moored not far from the beach. Painted on the hull one could read the name *Anne Louise*. From it two figures could be seen watching the beach: a man and a woman, she holding a pair of binoculars.

"I see Cris and the countess coming out of the house!" Desiree's excited voice narrated while her eyes remained glued to the binoculars. She veered to the right: "I see Robbie...he's walking out of that hotel, the Palace something."

Beside her, Spigot strained his eyes trying to see what was happening on the shore, as his binoculars had been unceremoniously confiscated from his hands. Meanwhile Max and John Laughton, each with a cold drink, sat on deck chairs under an awning.

"Copacabana Palace," her patient husband corrected.

"Yes, that one. Now...Cris and the countess stopped walking." A few seconds passed and Desiree resumed: "The countess is leaving and Cris is walking towards Robbie." Another interval. "They met! They are talking... Darn, it's too far to read their lips!"

"Even if you were near enough, since when can you read lips, old girl?" her husband asked.

"They are embracing. Oh, how romantic: they are kissing, Max! Yippee," she squealed, and jamming the binoculars into Spigot's eager hands, spun around and ran to her husband.

John Laughton turned to Bunky, who stood by silently with troubled eyes. "It seems to me that in the near future you might have the opportunity to, once more, help tame another little monster."

"*Non sum qualis eram*," said he in a colorless voice, with such a discomfited expression that caused both Laughton and Max to fall into a paroxysm of laughter.

Oblivious of everything else around her, Desiree plopped into her husband's lap, almost toppling his drink, and hugged him. "How much fun it will be, dear, *dear* Max! Can you imagine?" And not waiting for an answer, she stood up and started waltzing around, her face lit up with enormous joy while John Laughton watched, amused, and Bunky scowled. Then she suddenly stopped and became serious. "I must start planning our trip to Paris."

"Trip to Paris? Why are we going to Paris," was her husband's puzzled query.

"Trip to Paris," Spigot echoed, excited, and in his mind was already engaging himself to the travelling party.

"For Cristina's trousseau—what else? And Robbie must do something about a decent place to live. He can't possibly take Cristina to his apartment; it's appallingly small." She then turned wondering eyes to her husband: "What if they came to live at our hotel?"

## FINIS

# ABOUT THE AUTHOR

Emilia Rosa was born in California and raised in Brazil. During her childhood she lived in Rio de Janeiro, where every sunny weekend was generally spent at the beach. Having moved to South of Brazil, she holds fond memories of summer vacations spent with her married sister in Rio, which also involved many hours at the beach. Her love for the sea and Rio de Janeiro, as well as that city's history, permeates the pages of her first fiction book, Finding Cristina. During her teens she avidly read in Portuguese, Spanish, English, French and Italian. A few years ago she developed a love for murder mysteries written during the Golden Age of Detective Fiction. Emilia moved back to the United States several years ago. She has published poetry and is planning a sequel to Finding Cristina. Her readers can contact he

**Facebook, Instagram, Goodreads
Emilia Rosa Author**

## FOOTNOTES

[i] Natives of Rio de Janeiro.
[ii] 1920s slang: a sexually promiscuous woman.
[iii] Carnaval reveler
[iv] Rake
[v] Beco: Portuguese for cul de sac.

Made in the USA
Columbia, SC
12 February 2023

11758028R00100